When self-proclaimed good girl Jessica Knight literally bumps into apparent bad boy Connor O'Brien in a suburban Milwaukee wine bar, she is skeptical—of his intentions and the prospect for real love. A former priest, Saint Con is now a street lawyer for Milwaukee's homeless. After a night of sizzling romance, Jess begins to thaw, and in the days that follow, she is so charmed by Con that she allows herself to start falling in love. Unfortunately, on their first real date, Con fails to appear. Jess doesn't know if she's been ghosted or if Con was unavoidably detained, but she leaves their meeting spot devastated.

Until she discovers that Con is missing. Really missing. The police won't help because he's not a vulnerable adult, nor is there proof that he has been harmed. So it falls to Jess and her friends to find him. After surmounting numerous obstacles, Con is finally found, gravely injured and in a coma. Suddenly it appears a promising love match may be over before it really began.

Saint Con

ISBN: 978-1-4874-3978-1
Cover art by Martine Jardin

Published by eXtasy Books Inc

Look for us online at:
www.eXtasybooks.com

Saint Con

By

Seelie Kay

Dedication

To those who fight to house the homeless, feed the hungry, and heal those who have lost their way. You are my heroes!

Chapter One: Promises, Promises

"Oh, shit!"

Totally oblivious to her surroundings, Jessica Knight exited the wine bar restroom and slammed into a large, immobile object. Quickly, she stepped back and gazed up at said object. It took everything within her to squelch a gasp. The man blocking her path was the classic bad boy. Tatted arms, wild dark brown hair, a devil-may-care smirk, and intense blue eyes that were so fierce, she was sure he could see into her soul.

Dammit, he was hot.

The man studied her and chuckled. He reached down, removed the tube of lip gloss she still held in her hand, and pocketed it. "I've made a mess of your mouth." He shrugged, then leaned down and kissed her. "Hell, you're going to have to fix it, anyway."

Though brief, the kiss sent butterflies ping-ponging through her stomach. Jessica's hand flew to her lips, and she stared at him dumbly. "Uh huh." Normally, her response would have been outrage. Seriously, strangers did not just walk up to a woman and steal a kiss. That bordered on sexual assault. Yet this man had struck her dumb.

Jessica was a respectable lawyer. She'd put herself through law school working three jobs and surviving on apples, blue box macaroni, and tomato soup. She had worked hard and continued to do so, never once crossing the line onto the dark side. Until now.

She was the classic *good girl*. She learned the ways of the world at the feet of nuns at an all-girl's school. Actually, it was rather surprising she hadn't joined a convent. When she was fourteen, she had declared that intention. It was more out of fascination with the cafeteria food at her great aunt's Order than anything. But she discovered boys shortly thereafter and shifted gears. Still, her religious training stuck, and it influenced every decision she made. She didn't take unnecessary chances. She always played it safe. Especially with men.

She knew to stay away from men who were unbearably handsome, kissed like a seductive rock star, and were a member of some biker gang. Jessica stared at the man. He was all wrong for her. It didn't matter that a single kiss had her yearning for more or that she wanted to crawl up this man like a monkey. He was just wrong for her. *Step back, Jess. This guy is trouble.*

Jessica turned to move away, but he stopped her. "You're not running away after that, doll. You and me? We've got business to attend to. I know it. You know it. *Capiche*?" He grinned and leaned down to kiss her again.

Jessica fought the heat racing through her, the electric current melting her resolve and making her lady bits dance. This man kissed with expertise, igniting a passion previously unknown to her. Again she pulled back and stared at him. Her lips felt as if they had been seared with a branding iron. Slowly, she shook her head. "No. This is not happening. I'm not in the habit of kissing complete strangers."

The man grinned, his gorgeous blue eyes taking on a twinkle. "When you know, doll, you know. And I know that you and I belong together. When I saw you across the room, my heart lit up, and I knew we had to meet. And now, with a single kiss, I know we belong together. I know you feel it, too, but your brain hasn't caught up yet. Give it time. It will."

Jessica pinched her arm. Surely this was some sort of dream. A baffling, mad dream, born of too many romcom flicks and lonely nights spent consuming steamy romance books. This shit didn't happen in real life. Jessica didn't have time for a tumble between the sheets with an extremely handsome stud muffin. At least not when she was busting her ass to become professionally and financially solvent. Her rigid path made no allowance for a one-night stand, much less romance.

She stiffened her spine and glared at the Alpha before her. She motioned between the two of them. "You've got the wrong girl. I don't do one-night stands, and I don't have time for anything else." She scowled. "You're nothing more than a horny predator who stepped into my path, assuming I was easy prey." She tossed her hair over a shoulder and planted her hands on her hips. "Don't let this angelic façade fool you. I may look like a blonde green-eyed nymph with a body for sin, but inside I'm a lethal paragon of justice with claws that leave scars. So step aside, hot stuff. I want to get back to my drink."

The biker laughed and cocked an untamed eyebrow. "You did not just call yourself a lethal paragon of justice. My God, I thought I left all of those behind in law school." He continued to chuckle. "Arrogant much?"

Jessica felt her hackles rise. "You're a lawyer? No way. You're just too…too scruffy." Her eyes swept the man's muscular body. *Oh, my.*

The sexy smirk was back. "Let me tell you a secret, doll. Prior to law school, I was on my way to becoming a priest."

"No way," she repeated.

"Yeah. After a few years, I was advised that I was too independent and too liberal to serve the church. They also expressed doubt at my ability to live a celibate life." He shrugged. "That happened after I informed a certain instructor that I didn't *swing that way.*"

Jessica gaped. She must be dreaming. Her friends often joked that her perfect mate was a priest. This guy must be a figment of her imagination.

"You need to learn not to judge a book by its cover, doll, as I didn't judge you." He fingered her hair. "These blonde curls scream angelic, but your eyes scream warrior princess. And doll, I love a woman who breathes fire."

Jessica abruptly shook herself. "Now I know I'm dreaming. This is too fucking irrational to be real." She closed her eyes and mumbled, "Wake up, dammit. This isn't real. I'm just in a deep sleep caused by too much work and too little down-time."

The hunk touched her hand, and her eyes flew open. God, his very touch sent a thunderbolt of heat to her core.

"Let me introduce myself, doll. I'm Connor O'Brien, and you are?"

She gazed at him. "Jessica…Jessica Knight. Also a lawyer and…a former almost nun." She grinned. Jessica couldn't help it. She was dazzled by this man and even she could admit it.

Connor smiled. "You're my future, doll. I know it. We have a bright, exciting, sensual future ahead of us." He took her hand and led her to the bar. "Let's drink to that."

Jessica attempted to pull away from him, but he was not surrendering her hand, refusing to let it go. What the hell was wrong with her? Unwanted touching usually earned a kick to the groin. Why was she giving in, and so easily? Connor picked Jessica up off her feet and settled her onto a stool.

Her best friend, Sadie English, who had been waiting for her return, giggled. "I've heard about catching diseases from public toilets, but I've never heard about catching a man." A sly expression crossed her sweet face, and she extended her hand to Connor. "Hello, I'm Sadie. What apple cart did you fall off of?" She tossed her head of burgundy, pink-tipped curls, and her stylishly trimmed eyebrows pitched up over curious brown eyes.

Connor rolled his eyes as he took the stool next to Jessica. "Name's Con." He shook her hand. "Both lawyers?"

Sadie burst out laughing. "Hell, no. I enjoy my life. You won't find me trapped in some windowless office working sixty hours a week. I'm into bagels." Sadie pointed at the tee shirt she was wearing, bearing the words, *bagels are my everything*.

Con made a face. "Bagels?"

Sadie grinned. "My family owns *Bagels & More*. We make twenty kinds of bagels daily."

Jessica nodded. "Not just bagels, but bagelwiches and bagel cakes and stuffed bagels. My favorite is the egg-in-the-hole bagel."

Connor studied Sadie. "I think I know your father. Tall, thin, gray hair? Name of Jeb?"

Sadie stared at him. "How the heck do you know my father? I've never seen you in the store, and believe me, I'd remember."

"St. Ben's Social Justice Committee. I'm the chair."

Sadie's jaw dropped. "You're the guy with the traveling justice center? The guy who got kicked out of the seminary and became a lawyer?"

"Or, as your father claims, got dumped into the devil's lair."

Sadie bounced up and down on her stool, her eyes wide with excitement. "My God, I can't believe it." She grabbed onto Jessica to steady herself. "Jess, this is the guy I told you about. He travels around Milwaukee County offering legal services to the unhoused. In an old food truck." She bounced again. "And you have a motorcycle. You're a biker. Not *that* kind of biker, but a member of God's Warriors. You guys are *amazing*. You do so much good, but in secret." Sadie pounded on Jessica's back. "I can't believe he's *that guy*."

Jessica's eyes narrowed, and she stared at Con. "She's

kidding, right? You're not Saint Con." She shook her head in disbelief. Even she had heard of the guy. She nudged Sadie. "Trust me, he's no saint. He hit on me."

Con chortled. "What? You think you have to be celibate to be a saint?"

Sadie snorted. "Not looking like you." She made a sweeping motion with her hand. "This man is certainly a gift from God…and a gift to all women. Even God wouldn't waste all of this perfection on celibacy."

Jessica buried her head in her hands and moaned, "Time to cut you off, girl. All that tequila has turned you into a gushing, simpering fool."

Sadie hit her on the shoulder. "Better than a dried-up old spinster lawyer." She winked at Con. "Her girly parts have cobwebs."

Jessica's head shot up in horror. She gasped and slapped Sadie's arm. "You did not just say that." She grabbed Sadie's drink and moved it to the end of the bar. "You're done."

Con nudged her and winked. "No worries. I know how to remove cobwebs."

Jessica flushed. "Well, why…I mean, why should I care? It's not like you're going to remove…my, um, cobwebs." She sank onto her stool, too embarrassed to look at the man.

Con erupted with laughter. "Gotta love a woman who can still blush." He placed a finger under her chin and tilted her head up, then moved in for another kiss. "Doll, I promise I'll be gentle." He slid an arm around Jessica's shoulder. "Now, tell me, where do you work?"

"Downtown."

Sadie made a face. "At Brisby & Sutton, that stuffy old firm that handles the estates of Milwaukee's rich and famous. You know, the snobs with trust funds and money to burn. The kind of stuff that's so boring, it paralyzes the brain."

Con smiled at Sadie. "Why do I think you're the devil on

this woman's shoulder?"

Sadie laughed. "Because without me, Jess would live in a dusty old house, clothed in a decomposing wedding dress, bemoaning her lost youth."

Con cocked an eyebrow. "Are you sure you're into bagels? You should write sit-coms. You certainly have the patter for it." He grinned. "This gorgeous woman is no Miss Havershам. Besides, and from where I sit, bagels are just as boring as trusts and estates.

Sadie frowned. "Bagels are not boring. They are a gift that keeps on giving. I defy you to find one person who doesn't like bagels."

Jessica made a face. "I imagine there are thousands, maybe millions, who abstain. That's why they don't come into your dad's store."

"Ladies, let's not argue." He gently eased Jessica onto his lap and kissed her again. He handed her his phone. "Put your number in there so I can text you the details of our first date."

Jessica shifted uncomfortably on his lap. She shook her head. "Are you always this aggressive? You're behaving like I have no choice. I don't even know if I like you, much less want to date you." She stared at him defiantly.

Con tried to hide his amusement but failed. Once again, he brought her lips to his and kissed her. Deeply, thoroughly, skillfully.

When he finally pulled away, Jessica blinked, trying to clear the chaos in her head. Every single part of her body was on fire. She was clearly past the point of no return. She didn't believe in love at first sight, or insty-love, as her friends called it, but Jessica knew to the very depths of her soul that this man was her destiny. She wanted to drag him back to her house, rip off his clothes, and make love in every room, maybe even twice.

Sadie cleared her throat. "Uh, Jess, give him your number.

I've got to be at the shop by five in the morning. It's time to leave." She winked at Con. "Sorry, but I'm driving."

Jessica gazed at Sadie, then she gazed at Con. Her lips trembled. Tears misted her eyes. Suddenly, the thought of leaving this man was devastating. She had never had a one-night stand, but tonight that was clearly off the table. She didn't care about the risks, or the possibility she would never see this man again. All Jessica knew was that if she let him go now, she would regret it for the rest of her life.

As if sensing her indecision, Con lifted Jessica off of his lap and set her on her feet. He turned to Sadie. "If you don't mind, I'll take Jess home."

Sadie gaped. "Jess, are you sure? This is not like you. I mean, are you drunk or something? You just met this guy tonight. You don't do this kind of thing. What if…"

Con pulled out his wallet and opened it to display his driver's license. "You already know who I am through your father. I can assure you I am not in the habit of picking up women in bars. I just want to spend more time with Jess, and there's nothing wrong with that. In case you haven't noticed, there's something going on between us, and I'm not about to walk away from that." He slid one arm around Jess. "She will come to no harm, I promise you. But just in case I turn out to be a psycho, take a picture of my driver's license." He set his wallet on the bar for Sadie. "On the flip side, we're consenting adults, and whatever happens is between us."

Jessica nodded. "I'll be fine, Sadie. Just follow our protocol for first dates. And don't go overboard. Text in two hours, and if I don't respond, call. You know the drill." She nudged her. "I'll be fine."

Sadie sniffed. "This is so bizarre. I want to protect my best friend, but I also want this to be real. She deserves this."

Connor kissed Jessica's cheek. "And so do I."

Truth was, Jessica was less than comfortable allowing Connor to take her home.

Sadie was right. She wasn't that kind of girl. But this time, she was allowing her heart to rule her head. And her heart was telling her that this was right. She was overwhelmed by this man. Her heart was racing, her body was overheating, and her brain was freaking out. Jessica was completely enamored. How could that be?

Connor held onto her tightly as they walked to his car. A very nice late model car. Funny, she was expecting a rusted-out Beetle.

"What, no food truck? No motorcycle?"

Connor chuckled. "Both in my garage. A car is a much safer option at night." He opened the passenger door but stopped Jessica before she sat. "Just because I work with the homeless does not mean I've taken a vow of poverty. I like my creature comforts just like anyone else. I'm not some poor schmuck looking for a sugar momma." His gaze focused on her lips and his eyes lit up. Connor sighed. "Oh, lovely Jessica. You are my destiny. Cupid has lodged his arrow firmly in my heart. I don't care what happens tonight. I can assure you I will do everything in my power to make you mine." He kissed her gently. "I won't push. I won't beg. I won't demand. From now on, you're calling the shots. I am putting my heart in your hands."

Jessica stared at him. How the heck was she supposed to respond to that? With a shy smile, she moved into the passenger seat and peered up at him. "That's a lot of responsibility to foist on someone you just met. Trusting them with your heart."

"And I'm not even a bit worried."

Jessica sighed. "This whole situation is unreal. Please don't break my heart."

"All I can promise is that I will treat your heart with care."

Connor walked around the car and settled into the driver's seat. He motioned to his GPS. "Plug in your address and we'll be on our way." Jessica complied, and when the GPS activated, he laughed. "Wow, this will be a short trip. You're barely five minutes away."

Jessica shrugged. "It makes more sense to stick close to home when drinking. Besides, this is Oak Creek, we're headed to Franklin. Both set up drunk traps on weekends. I get paranoid, especially close to the end of the month."

"Are we headed to an apartment? A house?"

"My grandma's house." She gazed at Connor, and when he made a face, she snickered. "I don't live with my grandmother. I inherited the house after she died."

"Okay, but Franklin is, like, expensive. How can you afford it? You're what, twenty-five?"

Jessica chuckled. "Twenty-eight, and I can't afford it. The house is paid off, but the property taxes alone are killing me. And every year I'm reassessed, so they can pump those taxes higher. It's like they want to chase out anyone who isn't making the big bucks. Thank God for my roommate. Together, we can cover the taxes, food, and utilities."

Connor offered a slight smile. "So, you have a roommate?"

"Yeah, and she has a kick that could castrate a man. She grew up in the low-rent district in Minneapolis. She knows how to protect herself and also packs a taser. So beware and be wary." She lightly tapped his shoulder. "She shoots first, ask questions later. I wouldn't want to run into her in a dark alley." Jessica didn't tell him her roommate was currently in New York. No sense in making him too comfortable.

"I'll keep that in mind."

He pulled up to her home. She directed him into the driveway and led him into her home. Con passed through the front door and stopped. "Wow. This looks like a condo in Manhattan. Very chic."

Jessica chuckled. "My roommate is pretty handy, so we made a few changes to brighten the place up. New furniture, new paint, new fixtures. She took out a half wall. Now it feels like our home. Grandma lived here almost forty years. Believe me, it was time for a change."

Connor approached a sofa with big soft pillows for cushions. He sat and struggled when his body sunk in deep. A bemused expression crossed his face. "How do you get out of here safely? I feel like I've been swallowed up by foam."

"But you'll never have a sore butt." Jessica giggled. "And if you fall asleep on it, it's like snuggling up to a cloud." She bounced down next to Connor and cuddled up next to him. "Don't worry, if all else fails, I have a lasso around here someplace. I'll get you out."

Connor made a face at her. "A lasso? Really?"

"From my cowgirl days. I had the hat, the boots, the skirt, the whole enchilada." She smirked at him and shrugged. "But, hey, I was ten."

Connor laughed. "I'd pay for a photo of that." He pulled Jessica closer and traced her lips with a finger. "Later." Connor bent down to kiss her.

Jessica's eyes drifted closed and her hand went into his unruly hair. How could a man have such silky locks? It wasn't fair.

Connor's demanding tongue probed her mouth, then entangled hers in a sultry dance. Their kiss became heated, and before Jessica realized it, she was flat on her back. Connor tasted her neck while his hands gently explored her body, each touch igniting a flame within.

Their adolescent humping brought forth a tortured moan. Jessica wanted more. "You have way too many clothes on. I need to see you." Jessica tugged at Connor's jacket and tee shirt, finally separating them from his body. She ran her hands through the dark, curly hair that covered his chest.

Taking in the tattoos that ran up one arm, she licked and kissed her way to his shoulder, stopping to gaze at the angel that sat there. "How appropriate," she murmured. Jessica pushed Connor onto his back and licked the tattoo on the alternate shoulder, a devil with an inviting leer. Clearly, Connor was a man of contradictions. She wanted to consume him.

"My turn." Connor's eyes radiated heat as he pulled off Jessica's shirt and tossed it on the floor. He stoked her nipples through her lacy bra. "So pretty." He pushed the bra up and planted his mouth on her breasts, sucking each nipple until it was rigid and swollen. Connor's hands ran sensuously across her back, while his hips thrust his still-covered, swollen cock against her hot center.

Jessica writhed and groaned, desire racing through her. She wasn't new to sex, but she was new to the stunning need that enveloped her. She was barely conscious of unzipping her jeans and guiding Connor's hand into her panties.

Connor's fingers played with her pubic hair, then moved to her pussy. When he found her sopping wet channel, he groaned. "Damn. You're so wet for me." Suddenly, his fingers were everywhere, massaging her clit, stroking her G-spot, filling her pussy, while his lips sucked on her neck.

His thrusts increased in speed and force as Jessica's mind spiraled closer and closer to euphoria. Her body shuddered and bucked while she rode Connor's hand without restraint. With a shriek and a shudder, Jessica exploded. In a daze, she crawled up Connor's body and kissed him deeply.

Connor pulled her tightly against him, his body absorbing the aftershock of Jessica's orgasm. When she finally stilled, he chuckled. "I was not expecting that at all."

Jessica huffed. "Neither was I."

Connor absently stroked her hip. "I suppose it's time for me to go." He tried to sit up, but Jessica refused to move. Slowly, she lifted her head, her eyes glazed with pleasure.

"You're not going anywhere." She smiled at him. "Remember? I'm in charge."

He chuckled. "I got the impression you..."

Jessica ignored him. She ran her tongue over his tattoos, then kissed his chest and stomach. She continued to nuzzle his stomach while she tugged at the zipper of his jeans and wrestled his cock free. Her hand gripped him as she considered his penis. "Oh, this is so lovely." Her tongue circled the tip, and she moaned at the taste of him. Earthy, slightly salty, with just a hint of pepper. Addicting.

Connor's eyes closed and, and he emitted a soft hiss. "Doll..."

She ignored him as her tongue explored his girth. Jessica ran her tongue up and down his length, stopping to blow on the wetness left behind. His already rigid cock swelled and lengthened. Jessica sat back on her thighs and raised an eyebrow. "Still want to leave?"

Connor's gaze met hers, and he offered her a slight smile. "I think I changed my mind, but maybe we should move this some place more private? I'd hate to get tazed by your roommate if she walks in on us."

Jessica nodded and deftly crawled off Connor. She extended her hand and pulled him up from the sofa. They stared at each other for a moment, apparently both stunned by their sizzling connection. Finally, Jessica extended her hand and said simply, "Follow me."

Chapter Two: Possibilities

Jessica carefully sprayed olive oil on her half bagel and set it down in a frying pan.

As it sizzled, she cracked an egg and gently guided it into the center hole. Then she covered the pan and set the timer for three minutes. When the timer rang, she removed the cover, lifted the pan and slid the bagel onto a plate. Grabbing a bottle of balsamic vinegar, she made a thin swirl around the plate and moaned, "Perfection."

She placed the plate on her kitchen table and sat. Her body ached, but in all the right places. For a man who had once contemplated the priesthood, Con had some incredible skills in bed. He had ravished every inch of her body repeatedly. She had done things she didn't know her body was capable of. By the time his phone rang, she was wrung out, so exhausted that she could barely keep her eyes open as he explained he had to run to a Milwaukee police station. A client had been arrested after a violent encounter with a stranger at a homeless encampment under the freeway.

Despite her exhaustion, Jessica couldn't sleep after Con left. She was in a state of bliss. The way he touched her, ignited the fire within her core, was without equal. No man had ever made her feel like that. Her mind was filled with everything Con.

She had invited Con to return, but when dawn lit up her bedroom and her bed remained empty, Jessica threw off her blankets and stumbled into the kitchen. After three cups of coffee, her stomach started up with that troublesome gurgle and demanded food. Thank God it was Saturday.

Jessica forked into her egg-in-a-hole and swallowed slowly. In the light of day, she realized that her body and brain had betrayed her. Jessica's response to Con had been total capitulation. She had melted into him like a grilled cheese sandwich. There were no limits, only submission, and now it terrified her. Why him? Why now?

"Girl, what the heck is wrong with you? You look like you're about to slip into a coma." Jessica's roommate, Sydney, waltzed through the front door hauling an oversized suitcase. She dumped her luggage and hurried to the coffeepot, then filled a mug and sank into a chair, sighing dramatically. "Catching an early morning flight out of New York City is not for sissies. Even at that hour, the streets are clogged with traffic. I thought I'd miss my flight. But no way was I staying there another night. I paid the cabbie triple to get me the airport on time." She pointed at Jessica's plate. "Why can't you eat bacon and eggs like a normal person? That concoction is just sad."

Normally, Jessica would take offense. Or at least throw out some snark. Sydney was always criticizing her diet, which was easy when you were a seductive amazon. Jessica didn't have the energy to reply. Instead, she blinked and put down her fork. Then she made an agonized face. "Something happened last night." She pawed at her tangled hair, then emitted a disgusted sigh. *Great.* She actually had sex hair. Jessica tugged at the neckline of her sleep shirt. She was pretty sure Connor had marked her while they feasted on one another. Sydney would be all over that.

Sydney gasped. She grabbed Jessica's shirt and uncovered a few love bites. In a panicked voice, she shrieked, "Oh my God, did someone hurt you? Were you attacked? Do I need to get you to the ER or call the police?" She grabbed Jessica and hugged her. "Oh my God, Jess. Are you alright?" She rocked Jessica back and forth. "Oh, I'm so sorry. So sorry. Momma will fix this."

Jessica pulled away from Sydney and shook her head. Her eyes filled, and she sniffled. "No, it's not like that. No one hurt me. I'm just really overwhelmed and confused. Like I wandered into Willy Wonkaland and ate all the chocolate until I puked, then dived right in again."

"And he gave you hickeys?" Sydney's voice rose. "Jess, you're not making any sense. What the hell happened? Whose balls do I have to tase?"

Jessica picked up her coffee cup and took a long sip. She swiped at her eyes and nose. "Sadie and I went to that new wine bar in Oak Creek. I went to the bathroom, and when I walked out, I bumped into this man. Syd, he was dressed like a biker and all tatted up, but he was gorgeous. Scorching hot. I swear I could orgasm just looking at him. He grabbed me and kissed me and said something like I was his future."

Sydney chuckled. "So, you kneed him in the nuts per usual and hustled out of there? Right? Oh, sweetie. I'm so sorry. Men are such jerks."

A single tear rolled down Jessica's cheek, and she shook her head. "No, I kissed him again and then he sat with us at the bar and he turned out to be that saint guy who helps the homeless out of a food truck..." Jessica sobbed. "Then we came back here and we...we...Oh, I am so embarrassed. He must think I'm one loose goose. And now I'm sitting here wondering if I made a mistake and whether he's ever going to call me again. Oh God, I am such a loser. Why can't I just take this like a woman? Most would just move on."

"Wait a minute, you met Saint Con? Connor O'Brien?" Sydney banged her feet against the floor like a drummer. "Girl, he's so hot! Tell me everything."

Jessica stared at her roommate. "Wait, you know him?" She stopped. Of course Sydney knew him. Although they had been law school classmates, Sydney aspired to be among the elite in the business world. She'd majored in Mechanical Engineering as an undergraduate and got a law degree so she could run her own business. Sydney was an inventor. She had turned the basement in Jessica's home into a Maker's Lab, with state-of-the art equipment. When she wasn't off on a modeling gig, she was tinkering.

Syd had supported herself as a model since she was eighteen. People always said she resembled Beverly Johnson, the first black model to appear on the cover of *Vogue* in the nineteen seventies. Except her eyes were a musky green, courtesy of a white grandmother. Syd was tall and thin, confident and gracious. Everything you would expect of a top model, which she wasn't yet, but she had made enough money to put herself through school. Now she modeled to fund her passion, creating the next big thing.

Her bank account was flush, but Syd was thrifty. With the help of a financial adviser, she was building a portfolio that would fund manufacturing her inventions. She was halfway to her initial goal—a million dollars. Meanwhile, she rented from Jessica and hoarded most dollars earned. That Sydney knew Connor was a no-brainer. She was a networking machine, making connections wherever she went. Most likely she'd met Con at some high-society function. Unlike Jessica, Syd was a social butterfly. People loved her. She was smart, funny, and real. Men worshiped her and women wanted to be her best friend.

She and Jessica had bonded in law school when a certain Torts professor treated them like airheads. They'd formed their own study group, and when it became known they were at the top of their class, other students clamored to join. Most were refused.

Syd smiled. "Of course I know him. *You* want to know him. Not only is he charming and incredibly good-looking, but he does good just to do good. He doesn't want accolades or awards. He does good because it's the right thing to do. Plus he was top of his class at Yale. Has a big trust fund, which he spends to fund his mission. He's the total package."

"Yale? How did he wind up in Milwaukee? He should probably be on Wall Street."

Sydney chuffed. "And join his brothers, uncles, and father? Con will tell you he never aspired to wretched excess, he grew up in it. Why do you think he wanted to become a priest? Like me, he knows the value of a dollar, but he doesn't worship it."

"So, he dresses like a biker and kisses strange women in bars? That's a bit off."

"Oh, honey, have you looked in the mirror lately? You've got that whole pretty white girl thing going on. Connor goes after what he wants, and last night, he wanted you."

Jessica frowned. "So, it was lust-at-first-sight?" Her lips formed into a pout. "Well, doesn't that make me feel cheap?"

Syd laughed. "There is nothing about you that says *cheap*. You could pass for an angel. And angels attract saints."

Jessica waved her off. "Stop it. I'm a one and done. A pit stop on his path to glory. He rushed out of here this morning. Said nothing about seeing me again." She made a face. "What the hell did I expect? I meet this incredible man, willingly spread my legs, and we haven't even gone on a date yet. I don't know what came over me."

"Well, I imagine he did."

Jessica stared at her. "I can't believe you said that."

Syd shook her head. "You need to chill. For all you know, it could be one of those insty-love things. Love at first sight? He saw, he met, he conquered. Give the guy a few days to process. Chances are, he's wondering what happened just as much as you are. If you haven't heard from him by Tuesday, then you'll know. Guys are a little slow. In my experience, if they're going to ask for a date, it will be within four days."

Jessica groaned. "How the hell am I supposed to wait four

days?" She stood and pulled at her hair in frustration. "Last night was magical. No, it was a miracle. He wanted me for me. Then, poof, he's gone and I don't know if I'll see him again." She palmed her face. "Why was I so stupid?"

The doorbell rang, and Jessica's gaze moved to the front window. A florist's delivery van idled at the curb. She groaned. "It's for you, Syd. No doubt another admirer."

Sydney jumped up, obviously delighted. "Oh, goody!" She ran to the front door.

Jessica went back to her breakfast. Sydney kept the local florists in business. Not a week went by without an arrangement arriving at the door from some admirer. There was a bowl in the foyer filled with tip money for the delivery people. That saved Syd from having to search for her wallet. Most of Sydney's admirers sent roses. Jessica was allergic to roses. Thankfully, Syd was considerate enough to keep them in the basement.

Sydney skipped back into the kitchen holding a modest-sized vase, the flowers covered in butcher wrap. "They're for you," she sang. She plucked the card from the package and handed it to Jessica. "Open it."

Jessica frowned. "Who would send me flowers?" She opened the envelope and took out the card. "Last night was not an illusion…it was fate meeting destiny. Lunch on Tuesday? Con."

Sydney squealed. She ran to the living room and threw herself on the couch. She rolled over and thrust her legs into the air, shaking them with excitement. "I get to be a bridesmaid! My sister said I was too tall, my cousin said I was too distracting, and my aunt said they couldn't find a dress in my size, but you, Jess, you will ask me to be a bridesmaid."

Mildly amused, Jessica rolled her eyes. Sydney was Sydney. Passionate. Exuberant. Rose-colored glasses all the way. Jessica reached for the wrapped package and peeked inside.

Before she could open it entirely, her phone beeped. There was a text from an unknown number. "Sadie told me if I sent roses, I was signing my death warrant." Jessica squelched the butterflies that threatened to overwhelm her stomach. This man was too perfect. Perhaps his feelings *were* sincere. Maybe she wouldn't wind up a lonely spinster. Maybe this time, she'd finally find love.

Jessica wasn't a pursuer. Truth be told, she wasn't very good at romance. Most of the men she dated thought dinner bought them sex, so she never got past the first date. Sadly, she was the Queen of First Dates. There were seldom requests for more.

Con's flirty texts and delicious late-night phone calls left her befuddled. In three short days she knew everything about him, from how he broke his arm falling out of a treehouse to his favorite food, Shepherd's Pie. He learned about her mother's attempts to turn her into a prima ballerina, until she grew breasts, and about her lust for French Silk Pie. Con was intelligent, charming, sexy, and sweet. He truly was the whole package.

Jessica had to admit the man made her feel special. He made a point of praising her intelligence, her life choices, even her sense of humor. But did she make him feel special? Was she truly enough for him? Maybe he'd give her some hints at lunch. Because there was one thing Jessica was sure of. She could see a future with Connor O'Brien, and she did not want to mess that up.

Jessica took another sip of her iced tea and nervously watched the front door to Leaves Café, a salad restaurant.

Con was late. Almost a half hour late.

Jessica checked her phone. No messages. And she would have to leave soon. As an associate at Brisby & Sutton, she wasn't on the clock per se, but she was certain the uptight receptionist tracked her comings and goings. Whenever she was even a few minutes later, that woman glared at her, her disdain evident. She made Jessica feel like she was twelve.

Finally, Jessica gave up. With a sigh, she signaled her server. "I guess my guest is a no show. Can you wrap up a spinach salad for me? With the hot bacon dressing on the side and potatoes instead of croutons? And hold the mushrooms." The server nodded and left to put in her order.

Dammit, Jessica had been looking forward to this lunch. To seeing Con again. Maybe she had overestimated his interest, or maybe he just had cold feet. She sighed heavily. Why did every single man have to be a disappointment? Jessica really was better off alone. She'd thought Con was real. She was having feelings for him. Obviously, he did not share those feelings. The man might have the gift of Blarney, but obviously, he was not sincere. The server returned with her order, and Jessica headed back to her office.

She winced at the bright sunlight reflecting off the glass towers along Wisconsin Avenue. As she walked into the lobby of her building, her phone rang. She checked it. Sadie. She sent the call to voicemail. She probably wanted a report on the lunch date that had never happened. And she was not in the mood to talk about that. Her phone rang again. Syd. Again, she sent the call to voicemail. They could wait. She needed a few hours to throw herself a pity party. Too bad she didn't have any wine or ice cream to sulk in style. Her phone rang again and again. Jessica ignored all the calls. Then the texts started. Jessica turned her phone off and shoved it into her bag. *Enough. Let me wallow in peace.*

When Jessica exited the elevator to her floor, she sent a half-wave to the sour-faced receptionist and headed to the coffee station. At least she could whip up a double mocha latte on the fancy electronic barista machine. As she spooned beans into the grinder, her office mate, Taylor Green, walked in, swinging her empty coffee mug.

"Jessica, did you hear? There was some big shootout on the East Side. Some gang thing. The shooters got away, but there's a couple of people seriously injured. It's a mess. They locked down the U and an elementary school in the area. The police are going door to door trying to find the guys with the guns."

Jessica jammed in a filter, added the ground coffee, and hit the brew button. She shook her head. "I was out. Didn't hear a thing." She shrugged. "Kind of scary, though. There are a lot of places to hide. Dorms, apartments, houses. That's the reason I live in the burbs. It's safer."

When her coffee finished brewing, Jessica meandered back to her desk and fired up her computer. With a big sigh, she edited a brief she had drafted for a partner. Another contested will. Another family fighting over a decedent's final wishes. She couldn't imagine contesting her own parent's will. It was their money. Their property. They owed her and her three brothers nothing. They had the right to do as they saw fit. This job exposed the ugly underbelly of families. Too often, grief morphed into greed. Jessica had ensured her parents met with an attorney and executed an estate plan. She would have no further involvement until they passed.

While she reviewed the document, Jessica tried to shake off her disappointment at being stood up. Dammit. She had finally let down her guard, and Con took advantage. Men just couldn't be trusted.

Jessica worked steadily for several hours, pausing only when she heard multiple voices arguing outside her office. Was that Syd? Why on earth would she be at the firm? Jessica stood and walked out into the hallway. Syd and the receptionist were yelling at each other. "Um, Syd, what's going on? Why are you here?"

Sydney gazed at Jessica, and relief clouded her eyes. "Oh,

thank the Lord." She sniffed at the receptionist. "You can go back to work now. I found her." She made a shooing motion with her hands.

Syd grabbed Jessica and pushed her into her office. "Why aren't you answering your phone? I've been calling all afternoon, and so has Sadie."

Jessica shrugged. "I turned it off and put it in my purse. My date with Con was a bust, and I wasn't in the mood to discuss it."

Sydney glared at her. "Girl, your date was not a bust."

Jessica made a face. "Well, he didn't show up. I call that a bust."

"Jess, after the shootout, they found Con's truck nearby, trashed. Witnesses say the shooters ran from his truck and got into a fight with some gang further down the street. Everyone took cover when the bullets started flying. When it was over, Con…"

Jessica gasped. "What about Con?"

Sydney's eyes filled with tears. "Jess, Con is missing."

Jessica's mouth dropped open. "What do you mean, he's missing? I thought he was hurt."

Sydney shook her head. "No one knows what happened. Everyone's attention was on the shootout down the block. People pretty much sheltered in place. And when the police arrived, they searched Con's truck, but he was gone. They don't know if he went to the hospital, just wandered off, or was taken. He's just gone."

Jessica's heart dropped. "That makes no sense. Someone had to have seen something."

"We checked every hospital in the area. If he did head to a hospital, he never got there."

"I'm not following."

"Jess, he's missing. He just disappeared, and no one knows where he is."

Chapter Three: John Doe

Connor O'Brien woke up in a field.

A field that smelled like manure. Where the hell was he?

He closed his eyes and tried to remember. God, his eyelids hurt. *Focus.* Nothing made sense. The last thing he remembered was talking to some guy dressed in dirty pants and a holey shirt. The guy was unshaven, his hair greasy. Had he given him money? He couldn't remember. Then someone had hit him hard. The old guy? No, it wasn't him. Two kids demanding money. Con groaned. Every inch of his body ached. Clearly, those kids had beat the crap out of him. Why hadn't anyone stopped them?

Well, one thing was for certain. He wasn't in heaven. There was no pain in Heaven. So maybe he was in hell? No, that wasn't right.

Carefully, Connor turned his head and tried to assess his surroundings. He was lying in mud, amidst corn plants. Some were bent over with the weight of the ears, while others waved staunchly in the wind. Bees and flies buzzed about, and in the distance, he could hear what sounded like a plow. The sun was bright. It hurt his eyes. He shifted uncomfortably. Sweet Jesus, his body was imploding. He had never experienced such pain.

Connor moaned. He tried to sit up, but a sharp pain in his head forced him back down. Had that plow run over him? He couldn't remember. Con tentatively moved his legs. The pain was excruciating. He tried to bend his knees, but it was akin to moving thick tree stumps. Damn, was he paralyzed?

Again, he tried to sit up. This time, he got his torso off the ground. *Okay. Now let's try to stand.* Con attempted to push himself off the ground, but his arms collapsed and he fell back to the ground. Dammit. Why was he so weak? Connor sat up again and tried to take inventory. He was a mess. One knee was covered with dried blood, and his wrist was bruised and swollen. Again he attempted to stand. This time, he got to his feet. Although his body wavered, he stood up. Then his leg collapsed, and he fell back to the ground.

Connor closed his eyes. He fought to stay awake, but something was pulling him under. Finally, he gave in to the darkness.

The kick to his side roused him. "Hey, mister! What are you doing in my dad's field?" Connor's eyes opened, and he stared at a teenage boy.

The kid's face was filled with menace. "Kid, stop." He groaned loudly. "Just. Stop."

The boy scowled. "We don't let people sleep in our fields. When we run you over with the plow, you'll sue our asses off. I can call the sheriff, or you can just leave. If you need a place to stay, Mr. Miller up the street will let you sleep in his barn. You homeless guys have no business squatting in our fields."

Connor squeezed his eyes shut, trying to fight the pain in his head. "Not homeless," he mumbled.

The kid kicked Connor in the side again and pointed west. "Squatters. Two farms over. Now get."

Connor forced his swollen eyelids open and stared at the teenager. "Hurt. Need help."

"We don't help no stinkin' homeless. Get a damn job." The boy tried to grab Con's arm, but Con pulled away and flopped listlessly on the ground. He tried to move away from the kid, but he didn't get far. "Damn, are you drunk? Why can't you people get your acts together? Lay off the booze, get a job. Get a life." The kid spit into the dirt. "We don't need the likes of you in this county."

Con grabbed his head and tried to focus. Finally, he forced out a few words. "Call. The. Sheriff." He rolled onto his side and curled up into a ball. The last thing he remembered was the kid yelling. Maybe at him. Maybe at someone else. He no longer cared.

By the time the ambulance arrived at Morris Jackson's farm, the day had grown hot and muggy, not the best of conditions for an obviously injured man.

"You think I ran him over with the plow, Dad?" His son shifted nervously from foot to foot. His face turned red and his eyes misted. "Oh, God. I might have killed him."

Morris grabbed him and hugged his lean body. "Don't get your briefs in a bunch, Roman. That man looks like he was hurt elsewhere and dumped. He would be covered with mud if one of us had rolled over him, there'd be tracks, and well, he'd probably be dead. That guy isn't dead. Yet."

They silently watched emergency personnel lift the man off the ground and place him on a gurney. The sheriff at Morris. "Guy has no ID on him. No wallet. No phone. Keep a lookout. If you find anything, call us." He gazed at Roman. "Did the guy say anything to you, Ro? Give you any clue about who he was or what he was doing here?"

Roman shook his head. "No, sir. I thought he was one of those homeless guys, you know, one of those guys that gets dropped off by that bus from Milwaukee? He said he wasn't homeless. Told me to call you."

The sheriff frowned. "Those buses know to make drop offs only at Miller's farm. That's a good five miles from here. Too far for a man in his condition to walk." He tapped on Roman's shoulder. "You see anything, like a strange car or van?" He pointed to a nearby asphalt road. "I wonder…" He walked back toward the road, kicking corn stalks out of the way. He stopped and grunted. "There's some drag marks here." He pushed more stalks aside and bent over to search the ground. "And some footprints." He pulled out a phone and took a photo. "Morrie, I'm going to have to get an evidence tech out here to look around. I'm going to need you to hold off on working this area of the field for a few days."

Morris nodded. "I figured, but tell them to make it fast. This corn has to be harvested soon. My contract calls for delivery next week."

The sheriff sighed. "Believe me, I know it's not the best time to shut down your operation. 'Preciate you not squawking like Widow Anderson. If the guy had been found in her fields, she probably would have strung him up and fed him to her pigs. For someone who claims to be a good Christian, that woman is meaner than a rattlesnake."

Morris huffed and bumped against his son. "Ro had to find out the hard way. He and the Jeffers kid tried to cut though her fields, and she burned their asses with that durn BB gun. My wife wanted to drive over there with *her* BB gun and have an old-fashioned shootout. I convinced her neither she nor the old bitty would look good in prison orange."

The sheriff shook his head. "Just what I need. The Hatfields and the McCoys. He pointed at Roman. "And keep your friends away from here, too, Ro. I don't need them trampling the evidence. Someone roughed this guy up pretty bad, then dumped him. They probably thought he was dead. So at the very least, I've got an attempted murder on my hands. And if he dies, a murder. We're going to need all the evidence we can find to figure this out. No playing amateur detective, and no roosting in the crops to suck a blunt or whatever it is you kids do."

Roman flushed. "No, sir. We do that in…" His eyes grew

wide, realizing he'd just admitted to wayward behavior. He fell silent and peered at his father. "No, sir."

The sheriff chuckled. "Relax, Ro. Caught your dad in these fields in a time or two when he was a boy, and he wasn't getting high, he was getting busy with Emmy Lou Johnson." His face broke into a grin.

Roman stared at Morris. "Mom? You dragged Mom into a cornfield, too?" He slapped at his father. "That's disgusting."

Morris and the sheriff laughed. The sheriff punched Morris on the arm. "She was the prettiest girl at Central High, and this guy made sure everyone knew who she belonged to. Why do you think he married her the minute they graduated?"

Roman's mouth dropped open and he mumbled, "So embarrassing." He pulled at the hair on his head and shuddered. "I don't want to think about it."

The sheriff grinned. "Give it a year or two. You'll understand." He trimmed his hat, then slapped his leg. "Well, I'd better get back to the station, check on any missing persons or incident reports. Someone has to know who this guy is. He doesn't appear to be homeless, and his shoes are too new, expensive. I'm hoping he's already been reported missing."

Roman screwed up his face. "What happens if there is no missing person report?"

"Then he goes into our system as John Doe, at least until he wakes up and can tell us his name."

"And if he doesn't wake up?"

The sheriff clapped Roman on the shoulder. "We'll cross that road when we come to it. This kind of thing is a waiting game. Sometimes families wait a while before reporting a missing person, especially if they've gone off before. And other times, the family doesn't know the person is missing because they aren't in regular contact. Usually, it's not until someone raises a stink that we'll look. We don't always have the resources to conduct a search, but I can at least put his vitals into the system and hope the description pops for someone."

Roman studied the sheriff. "That sounds kind of inefficient."

The sheriff shrugged. "Missing adults, especially if they're not locals, aren't a priority. We have AMBER Alerts for minors, Silver Alerts for seniors, and Endangered Missing Persons Alerts for those who are impaired, but there are no alerts for average men or women missing from everyday walks of life, at least in Wisconsin. We don't have the budget, so that's just the way it is. Even after a missing person report is filed, it takes time to organize a search or begin an investigation. That's done locally, and as far as I'm aware, we have had no reports in the past few weeks. He could be missing from anywhere—Milwaukee, Madison, or Chicago, or anywhere in between. We're hampered by a lack of information." He tugged his hat. "Pray someone reports this guy missing and it's entered into NamUs, the national clearinghouse for missing persons. That's his best hope."

Morris side-hugged his son. "Anything we can do to help, Sheriff?"

The Sheriff adjusted his tool belt. "Not much anyone can do until he wakes up or the hospital releases a photo. Problem is, there are all sorts of patient confidentiality laws we can't breach. Like I said, this could turn into a real waiting game." He paused. "It can't hurt to ask around, though." He nodded at Roman, "Maybe one of your friends saw something or knows someone who's missing. You never know. Usually, people don't know what they know until you ask."

Jessica stared at the television. She had taped all the news reports on the East Side shooting and scoured the internet for related stories. There were so many versions of what actually occurred that it was difficult to get to the truth.

The shooters—who were apprehended trying to break into a nearby student dorm—claimed that they never attacked Con or his truck and didn't even know who he was. They also claimed the shoot-out at the convenience store wasn't a robbery, but a dispute with a local gang infringing on their territory. The two boys remained in custody, but they'd clammed up once their public defender was called.

Witnesses claimed they had seen the boys rough up Con, leaving him unconscious, but they had run for cover once the shooting started. No one could tell the police what happened to Con after their attention was diverted.

The police found nothing but trashed files and a smashed donut on the floor of Connor's food truck and a what could be a drop of blood—or raspberry jam—on the sidewalk. Since there was no blood trail, the police concluded he had gotten a ride elsewhere, but without witnesses, they couldn't confirm that. There was no evidence of foul play, no reason to investigate further.

"Where are the people with their phones, recording every little thing to post on Instagram or TikTok?" Jessica muttered. "A man doesn't just disappear into thin air. If he was there, where did he go? And if he wasn't there, why hasn't he shown up elsewhere?"

Sydney plopped down on the couch next to her and offered Jessica a sundae. Without thinking, Jessica grabbed it and shoved a spoonful into her mouth. "Oh my God, that's Bailey's fudge sauce and crushed thin mint cookies and pretzels and caramel and everything. This is wicked."

Sydney preened. "I know. I made it myself. Bought the custard from Ollie's up the street and mixed in stuff I found in our cupboards." She burped daintily. "I finished mine, but I'm still hungry. So if you can't finish that, pass it over."

Jessica pulled the sundae away from Syd. "Not a chance,

sista. My brain needs food." She nodded at the television. "I can't figure this out. First, Con stands me up, then he disappears. That makes no sense. I am so hideous that he had to leave the country?"

Syd laughed. "I think you're giving yourself too much credit. Besides, Con never struck me as a runner. He wouldn't stand you up. He'd tell you he changed his mind." She frowned. "Our problem is getting the police involved. I realize their budgets have been cut, so they don't have the funds or personnel to launch an immediate investigation, but the delay sucks. If he was hurt, I doubt he walked away, and for the life of me, I can't believe he was kidnapped. Sure, his family has money, but Con didn't advertise that. He dresses down so he won't intimidate the people he helps. I didn't know he had money until I saw him in a tux that clearly wasn't a rental. It was tailor-made. Then there's that fancy car of his. How many street lawyers drive a Lexus?"

"So, where the hell is he?"

Sydney shrugged. "He's not answering his phone and one of his friends checked his house on the south side, but no one came to the door. There was mail in his mailbox, and his car was in his garage, so maybe he went home to New York. Maybe there was a family emergency, and he panicked."

A flush of guilt hit Jessica. She was so pissed Con had stood her up that she never considered that it had been out of his control. When he didn't show up at *Leaves,* she had written him off and prepared to move on. She'd been angry and hurt, and if she was being honest, devastated. Sure, she didn't know Con well, but she felt a rare connection to the man. He checked all the boxes for a good match, maybe even a perfect one. His rejection of her made her lose hope. Hope that she would ever find a partner who suited her. "Not answering his phone sounds kind of ominous."

Sydney made a face. "Well, yeah. Like he lost his phone or

someone took it from him."

"So, what's next? Do we just wait?"

Sydney grabbed Jessica's melting sundae and took a bite. "Maybe not. I met his brother once. He gave me his number. Maybe I should call and see if he's been in touch with Con."

"Please. I'm slip-sliding between anger and fear here, and it's not a pretty place. Part of me wants to chew nails, while the other wants to vomit. I need to know what we're dealing with."

Sydney pulled out her phone and scrolled through her contacts. She tapped on something and put her phone on speaker.

"Dan O'Brien."

"Danny, it's Syd, from Milwaukee. We met at your brother Con's fundraiser last year."

"Syd, that luscious dish of ebony?"

Jessica rolled her eyes. The man's voice was deep and smooth. Unlike his brother, he sounded like a player.

Syd grinned and responded, "That's me, Danny."

He growled. "What's shaking, baby?"

Jessica scrunched her nose. Con's brother sounded like he didn't have a care in the world.

Sydney cleared her throat. "I'm sorry to bother you, Danny, but have you heard from Con?"

"Nope. Why? What's he done now?"

Sydney stared at the phone. "You didn't hear?"

"Hear what?"

"Danny, Con is missing."

"No, he isn't. I just spoke to him last week. He was all tied up in knots over some girl he had met. Kept saying she was *the one*. I told him was an idiot. All those years of deprivation must have skewed his *femdar*."

Syd tugged at her hair, the astonishment showing on her face. "His what?"

"His femdar—you know, his ability to assess women."

Jessica shook her head and mouthed, "What a tool."

Syd glared at the phone. "Whatever. The bottom line is, witnesses saw Con getting beaten up, but then a shooting occurred up the block, and while everyone's attention was diverted, Con disappeared. Danny, we can't find him. He's just gone. I was hoping maybe he was with you or your family."

Dan remained silent. When he spoke, his voice was shaky. "Um, I don't know what you're talking about. I have to go." There was a click and the Sydney's phone fell silent.

Jessica gazed at Syd. "What the hell? I can't believe someone hasn't contacted him. Surely his family knows. Why didn't they…"

Sydney held up her hand. "This is weird." She turned to Jessica. "Isn't this weird? He acted like he knew nothing. That family is really tight. That make no sense. Unless…"

"The police didn't take the witnesses seriously or any of the other people reporting him missing." Jessica threw up her hands. "So his family was never contacted. That's why there was no news. The police aren't pursuing his case. They don't believe he's missing. What a complete fuck-up."

Sydney's phone rang. "Danny." She swiped at the call. "Hi, Danny. I'm sorry…of, hi Mr. O'Brien…and Finn…No, it wasn't a joke. We're sure he's missing. At least, we can't find him. We've been calling his phone. No answer. His truck had some blood in it, but he wasn't there either. The police searched the immediate area but turned up nothing. Friends went to his house. His car was there, but he wasn't." She paused. "I'm not sure, sir. I know they were contacted. I'm at a loss…yes, sir." She waited. "Danny, please call me when you get here. I'll round up some of his friends to help." Sydney disconnected and shook her head. "Con's family didn't have a clue. How is that even possible?"

Jessica winced. "I thought Con was a public figure. Surely the police did a wellness check after he went missing. I thought that was standard procedure when someone disappears."

Sydney shook her head. "In this area, we're used to this kind of incompetence when you're black. But Con is white, a public figure, and rich. Maybe they found him and aren't releasing the information until they contact the family?"

"Except the family hasn't been contacted, so what is going on?"

"I have no earthly idea."

Chapter Four: Seventy-Two Hours

When Dr. William Wood walked into Con's room at Burlington Memorial Hospital, he stopped short.

Although his patient was in a medically-induced coma, two people of unknown origin stood over him, as if expecting the man to speak. Dr. Wood scowled and barked, "What are you doing to my patient?"

One man, dressed in a suit that could only come off the rack, flushed and stepped away. "We wanted to question him, find out who he is, maybe get a name so we can contact next of kin."

Dr. Wood exploded. "Step back from my patient." He strode over the men and pushed them back from the bed. "Now, who the hell are you, and how did you get into this room? The sign on the door clearly says *no visitors.*"

The second man, wearing a green sweater and brown slacks, pulled a wallet out of his pocket and flashed a gold shield. "Detective John Bronson, from the Burlington P.D. The Sheriff's Office contacted us about the John Doe, wanted to see if we could help identify him." He pointed to his partner. "This is Detective Hal Gunderson."

The doctor glared at him. "Your jobs don't justify illegally entering my patient's room."

Bronson frowned. "The nurse told us he was in a coma. We just wanted to look and see if he was someone we knew. She said it was okay." He made a face. "We didn't sneak in. We asked. Besides, with all the bandages around his head, and what looks like considerable swelling, there's no way to identify him. He's in a coma 'cause of brain swelling, I assume?"

"And some internal injuries we're hoping will start healing." The doctor took a deep breath. He knew the police were just trying to help. He just didn't like any strangers entering patient rooms. Even people in a coma deserved privacy.

The detective nodded. "When can we check back? Standard procedure for a John Doe is to get a photo and send it to area PD's. Maybe the DCI. If this guy isn't from around her, Criminal Investigations may have to take over."

Dr. Wood shrugged. "Well, he's healing, but no way to tell when his brain or face swelling will subside, at least enough to identify him. We tried to find some skin features—scars, birthmarks, tattoos—to help identify him, but he was so bruised, we couldn't really find anything helpful. There are some tattoos on his arm, but they're a real mess." Dr. Wood winced. "When that arm heals, I'm not sure how much will be intact. Also, what looks like an angel on one shoulder, a devil on the other. There's also evidence of a left arm fracture, probably from when he was younger."

"Any idea of age?"

"Late twenties, maybe early thirties. Hard to tell with all that facial swelling. But his body is muscular and toned, with no softening indicative of someone in middle age. His organs, heart and kidney, liver are in decent shape."

"Any defensive wounds?"

Dr. Wood nodded. "This guy fought back. Numerous abrasions and lacerations on all extremities. Looks like it was more than one attacker, though. He took one hell of a beating. If he survives, he is one lucky guy."

"If?" Bronson cocked an eyebrow.

"He's still in critical condition, which is why he's in a medically induced coma. Fortunately, every day he lives is a step toward a full recovery." He sighed. "I just wish we could identify him. He has to have family out there. The support of loved ones plays such an important role in recovery."

Bronson studied Con's face. "Any way we can get an eye color, Doc?"

"Blue. We had to check his eyes when assessing his condition. A deep blue. Not particularly unusual, but they might spark recognition among the right people."

"Or the wrong ones." Det. Gunderson's expression was thoughtful. "This guy was clearly attacked. I wonder if there is any way they'll return to finish the job?" He gazed at his partner. "Do we need to request heavier security?"

Bronson winced. "We're stretched tight as it is. It would have to be hospital staff."

Dr. Wood made a face. "Might be better off putting him in a room with cameras. We use those for patients who require round-the-clock observation."

Gunderson nodded. "That's the best we can hope for. Please brief the staff to keep their eyes peeled for any suspicious visitors and keep that *no visitors* sign up." He smirked. "And tell the nurses to enforce it."

Con didn't know where he was.

It was as if he was trapped in a world of sponges. They weren't smothering yet, but they kept him cocooned in nothingness. It was a strange sensation. He couldn't see forward or backward. All he could see were the damn sponges.

He tried to blink. Maybe that would clear his mind. But he couldn't remember how. *Think, Con. Open your eyes, then close them. Rapidly. Come on, you can do it.*

Con tried to squeeze his eyes closed. God, why was it so hard? *Blink, dammit.* Suddenly, his vision cleared, and the sponges faded away.

A blonde woman in a flowing white gown beckoned. "Come on, darling. I have a treat for you." She smiled. "A very sweet treat." She giggled. "Come on, let's go." She turned and walked away."

Con stared at her. "Wait. Who are you?"

She turned and smiled. "Why, I'm anyone you want me to be. This is your dream, after all." Suddenly, someone or something grabbed the woman and pulled her out of his line of vision. She struggled. Oh, how she fought her attacker. Then she screamed. "Help me, Connor. Don't let them…" the woman screamed again and was yanked away. With a loud *pop!* she disappeared.

"Uh, Miss? Are you there?" Con winced. The woman was gone. His eyes roamed the vast tunnel he was in. Was there no one else? *Pop!* His mother appeared. "Thank the Lord, Ma. Finally, someone I recognize. It's been so long." He smiled. "But you're always there when I need you. I need you now, Ma. Help me get out of here. I'm stuck."

An evil smirk formed on his mother's face. "Why should I save you, you dirty bastard? After all of your whoring around?" She spat at him. "I can't believe my son is such a deviant."

Con frowned. What on earth was she talking about? "Ma, I don't understand."

She cackled. She reached behind her and pulled out a young woman. The woman was beautiful. Angelic. Her blonde curly hair framed a petite face with luminous green eyes and sweet pink lips. The young woman struggled to free herself from his mother's grasp, but she slapped her, hard.

Con gasped. "Ma, what are you doing?"

His mother's eyes flared. They grew wider and wider, changing from green to a vibrant red. Her other features morphed as well. Her red hair evolved into writhing snakes, and her body twisted into a mishappen beast. Saliva dripped from malformed teeth. "I will kill her," she hissed. "She dared to taint my precious son, and for that, I will kill her."

Con moved closer. "No, Ma. I don't even know her." He stared at the poor woman. She was terrified.

Suddenly, a large saber appeared in his mother's hand. Slowly, she lowered it and nestled it against the woman's neck.

"No, Ma! Don't hurt her. I'll be good." Con dropped to his knees, pleading. Tears dripped from his eyes. "Please, don't hurt her. She has done nothing wrong."

His mother huffed. She lifted the saber and with a decisive swipe... *Pop!* His mother and the woman disappeared.

Pop! A glamorous dark-skinned woman appeared, dressed in a tight, metallic gold dress, the air around her filled with a thousand glittering stars. She smiled at Con as she waved her wand. She giggled. "The old bat. She was always butting in where she's not wanted. Thinks she can just enter my realm and snatch one of my subjects." She sniffed. "No one messes with Queen Sydney. No one." She pointed her wand at Con. "What the hell, Con? Why are you stuck down here? There's a beautiful world out there." She winked. "Along with your luscious lady love, Jess."

Puzzled, Con made a face. "Who's Jess? I don't think..." He shook his head vigorously, trying to remember. "Have I met her?"

Queen Sydney pursed her lips, then laughed. "Of course you have, silly. You're in love with her."

A sharp pain burrowed into his brain and Con seized his head with both hands. "I don't remember," he muttered. "I don't remember."

Pop!

John O'Brien and his sons, Daniel and Finn, entered the Milwaukee Police Department Administration Building.

The young woman seated behind the counter jumped up and scurried toward them. "Yes, sirs. What can I do for you?"

She shifted nervously.

John was well aware of the effect he and his handsome sons had on women and men. His wife, Moira, playfully called it *The O'Brien Mystique.* His face assumed a stern, intimidating expression. "We have an appointment with the Chief. Chief Porterhouse, I believe. The name is O'Brien."

"Yes, sir." The receptionist went to her desk phone and made a call. She turned back to them. "His admin will be out shortly. You can have a seat." She nodded at a set of worn chairs set up against a wall.

John harrumphed. "Where you shackle perps? Not likely, my dear." He pointed to a table with chairs in a nearby conference room. "We'll wait over there." Without receiving permission, he and his sons strolled into the room and sat.

Dan shot him a look of annoyance. "Geesh, Dad. Cut the little dictator act. Maybe that works with Ma, but these people don't know you from a hill of beans. We need their help. Can you hold off offending them until later?"

John chortled. "Oh, stop being a wuss. It never hurts to show people who's really in charge."

Finn shook his head. "Don't blow this, Dad. Dan's right. We need their help, and we may have to kiss their ass to get it. So get out your Chapstick and pucker up."

John slugged Dan's shoulder. "Oh, relax. I'm sure this is all much ado about nothing. If anything, Connor's off communing with some monks or something. He spends enough time praying and meditating for all of us."

Dan slapped his hand on the conference table. "Then why bother to come, Dad? If you're not as worried as the rest of us, why not stay home?"

John's face flushed, and he swiped at his brow. He muttered, "Because your mother called me a prick for wanting to stay home." He shook his head. "When that woman gets a bee up her bonnet..."

Finn groaned. "Nice, Dad. Blame it on Mom. Would it kill you to show a little affection for your youngest son?"

John's eyes narrowed. "What do you mean? I love all of my son's—equally."

Finn burst out laughing. "Be real. When Con got kicked out of the seminary, you were royally pissed and you didn't hide it. What is it about Irish families? Why do all of them think they must dedicate one child to the service of God?" He smirked. "Is it because the Irish are the worst sinners? Are you trying to buy your way into heaven by sacrificing one child to God?"

John felt his anger building. "I was not angry when he was booted by the priests. It was embarrassing. And for your information, the Irish have a long history of dedicating a child to the service of God. Back then, it was more to manage the cost of a raising a large family. Sending a child off to the convent or seminary eased the burden of feeding and clothing the rest."

Dan snickered. "So that's why we have so many priests and nuns in our family? It seems to me if you want to manage the cost of a large family, the best solution is not to have one. Fuck the rhythm method. Use birth control."

Finn made a face. "Which was illegal in Ireland until nineteen seventy-nine and then available only for family planning purposes. So, what's your excuse, Dad? You hardly needed to send a child off to their divine doom. Poor Con could have been spared all the bullshit."

Their father rolled his eyes. "As I remember it, the priesthood was Con's idea. Remember when he used to play Mass? He'd line you up and serve you communion with those soup crackers. And the wine. Damn, the three of you sure could guzzle that grape juice. Your poor mother was worried you'd inherited the curse of the Irish."

Dan laughed. "You mean our tendency to drink and be

merry? Funny how that turned out. Con's the only one who will touch alcohol and then he's one and done. Drinks apple juice because it looks like whiskey." He shook his head. "And Finn has never touched the stuff."

Finn shrugged. "All my friends are straight edge. None of us touch anything that will poison our bodies, no smoking, drinking, or drugs." He flexed his arm. "Fit as a fiddle and living past a hundred."

"With millions in the bank to boot." John chuckled. "Now if one of you would settle down and give your mother grandchildren, you'd be perfect."

Finn grinned. "Yeah, well, straight edge does not mean we're down on marriage. Maybe when I'm in my forties."

There was a knock on the door and a red-headed woman stuck her head in the door. "Gentlemen, I'll escort you to the Chief's office. He's ready for you now."

The three men stood and followed her out of the room.

"No one has officially filed a missing person's report for a Connor O'Brien. Even if they had, we would wait seventy-two hours to investigate, unless there is proof a crime has occurred. That's the long and short of it." Chief Porterhouse leaned back in his chair and steepled his manicured fingers. "Right now, we have nothing to go on, so our hands are tied." His ebony face was kind, but stern.

John 'O'Brien bristled. "That makes no sense. I was told that my son was beaten up by a couple of kids while in his truck. Those kids then ran up a street and shot up a convenience store. By the time they were in custody, my son was gone."

Dan leaned forward. "We were told the police searched the area and found nothing. Is that true?"

Chief Porterhouse opened a thick file set in front of him and paged through it. "I read this report before you came in.

A search of the immediate area found no evidence of your son and no evidence of a crime."

John frowned. "What about the witness reports? They saw those punks beat up my son."

The Chief shook his head. "Two of those witnesses were vagrants. They are notoriously unreliable. Most of their stories are enhanced by the bottle. They claim they saw a man get attacked, but they couldn't identify him. The third was an older woman who couldn't confirm what the vagrants saw. She witnessed the two kids running from the truck. That's it. Again, the police did a preliminary search, but found nothing and had no reason to continue searching."

Finn stroked his chin. "How big was the search area?"

"The perimeter was set by the site of the main incident, which was the shooting. All searches were related to confirming the events leading up to that. By the way, the two boys arrested deny the beating and we have no evidence to contradict them." The Chief sighed. "The district attorney is sorting through the evidence they collected and is preparing charges, none of which concern your son." He shook his head. "I'm sorry. The DA makes decisions based on evidence, and as it concerns your son, we have nothing."

John ran a hand through his hair. 'What do you suggest we do?"

"As I understand it, we're dealing with a white, able-bodied man. He possesses none of the triggers required for us to launch an immediate alert or investigation. We need evidence that he is truly missing or was harmed. Get that and we can move. If he doesn't turn up within seventy-two-hours, then file a missing person's report."

John cocked an eyebrow. "Isn't it a fact that the first seventy-two hours are critical when someone goes missing? Your rules seem contradictory. If it was your son, would you wait?"

"Hell, no. I'd have volunteers shagging the bushes,

handing out and posting flyers with his photo. I'd interview area store owners and nearby residents, including the vagrants. I'd get the information on social media and on the local TV stations. I'd also check out any place he frequents, including his home, churches, taverns, and the like. In my experience, people don't just disappear. They have to be somewhere.

"If you're lucky, he'll show up on his own. If not, you need to find someone or something that suggests a crime has been committed. You need to bury people in information so everyone is looking for him. If something happened, someone must have seen something."

John gazed at Dan. "That woman who called, the one who has a man's name? Think she can help? This isn't our city. We need a local guide."

Dan nodded. "Yeah, she's already offered, but I think we also need to call in the family. Our relatives know Con, so they have more of a stake in finding him."

Finn made a note on his phone. "I can make reservations at a hotel for anyone who shows up and find a suite for us. Obviously, we need to be prepared to stick around for a while."

John considered. "I'd better call your mother. She and her sisters will be a big help in taking care of the volunteers. Besides, she won't tolerate staying home while we're searching for Con." He gazed at the Chief. "I think we're going to need an extended-stay hotel. Any recommendations?"

"I'm sure my admin can give you some names. There are several in the suburbs."

The Chief stood and stuck out his hand. "If you find any evidence that he was kidnapped, or worse, call us immediately. If he is still missing after tomorrow, file a *Missing Persons* report. I'm sorry. It's not a perfect system, but we have to prioritize to best utilize the resources we have."

Dan gazed at him. "I get it, but I don't have to like it." He turned and walked away.

John shook the Chief's hand. "Thanks for your time. Everything inside me is telling my son is missing, and with or without your help, we *will* find him."

Finn also extended his hand. "I apologize for my brother's rudeness, but we're talking about family here. He's upset. We'd appreciate any help you can provide."

Chapter Five: The Tracking Chip

Sydney did not wait for the police to search for Con. She went through her contact list and organized a neighborhood search. Syd led two dozen people through the area where Con's truck was found. She had flyers displaying Con's face, description, and Jessica's pre-paid phone number.

They searched the nearby woods, knocked on doors, visited businesses, posted flyers, and questioned anyone they could.

A local bakery owner told Syd, "Saint is in the neighborhood on Tuesdays. He purchases a raspberry paczki and coffee, then sits on the bench outside of my shop." Paczkis, a filled fried donut, were most in demand on Fat Tuesday, but were enjoyed year-round. "Then he waits. Sometimes, ten guys show up, sometimes only two. But he's here like clockwork every Monday."

"So he was here on Monday, the day of the shooting?"

The baker nodded. "Sure was. Bought a dozen paczkis. Said he was expecting a crowd but had a date with a beautiful woman at noon, so he planned to leave the donuts with a note that said he'd return later. We had a big laugh about old Squeezer. That dude shows up every Monday. Takes a donut, then wanders off. Then just when Saint closes up, he reappears and asks if there's any leftovers." The bakery owner pointed to the alley where Con's truck was found. "We figure he sleeps in the alley back there. He must keep close watch, because he always shows up for extra donuts."

"So, he was there on Monday? Before the shooting?"

"Sure was."

Sydney started moving toward the alley. "He lives over here?"

The baker shrugged. "No idea. Only see him on Mondays."

Sydney thanked the man and asked a few volunteers to help her search the alley. They searched in and around dumpsters and peeked into garages and backyards but found no sign of the vagrant named Squeezer.

"Maybe he only shows up to get a free donut from Con and lives elsewhere," a volunteer mused.

"Or maybe he saw something and ran," said another.

"It doesn't matter why he's gone." Sydney blew out a frustrated breath. "He was most likely here on Monday and knows what happened. We need to find him. Where else do the homeless hang out?"

"Mainly the area shelters, some of the downtown churches, and when it's warmer, the parks," a female volunteer offered. "Of course, they also move around to get food." She gestured to a young volunteer. "Joshua, who offers free meals these days?"

Joshua tapped on his phone and his eyes rounded. He held up the screen. "Over a dozen sites near downtown, I'm sure there's more in the suburbs." He frowned. "Did you say the guy's name is Squeezer? As in Squeegee? That group that tries to clean the windshields on the cars stuck on Clybourne Avenue, waiting to get on the freeway?"

Syd gazed at him. "I thought the police put a stop to that."

Joshua laughed. "Like that works. The police run them off and they're back the next day. A few blocks over. But he could be with that crew. We found nothing that tells us he sleeps around here. I'm guessing he moves around, goes where the food or the money is."

"Which just makes our job harder." Sydney screwed up her face in thought. "Let's finish up posting these signs, then we can split up and hit some of the meal sites, as well as the squeegee gang. Show them Con's photo. Most will know him. Then ask about Squeezer. He's gotta be around here somewhere." She pointed at Joshua. "Take some of these flyers back to your dorm, maybe post them where students gather at the U. A lot of those students hang out around here. Maybe someone saw something."

"And tomorrow?" A teen-age girl asked.

Sydney slowly shook her head. "We keep on looking."

John O'Brien pulled his rental car to the curb and gazed at the house he'd been directed to.

On the lawn was a big sign that said simply, *Find Con Headquarters*. He grunted. "I guess this is it." He and his sons exited the car and made their way to the front door. It was flung open before they reached the porch.

A curvy blonde woman studied them. "You must be Con's family. I can see him in all of you." She opened the screen door. "Come on in. It's a little crazy around here, but Syd's got everything organized." She held up a phone. "I'm in charge of the tip line and making sure none of the volunteers walk off with my furniture." She turned to lead them inside. "I'm Jess, by the way."

Dan cleared his throat. "As in Jessica? Jessica, the woman Con has declared, is *the one*?"

Jessica rolled her eyes. "Well, that's yet to be determined. I'm not so sure about this love at first sight stuff." She shrugged. "Con stood me up on our first official date. Of course, if that hadn't happened, we wouldn't know that he was missing." Jessica's hand swept the room. "As you can see, we have people producing more posters, others manning social media sites and following up on any leads. People are calling every hospital and urgent care clinic within a one-hundred-mile radius."

John nodded. "Have you gotten anything yet? Any clues? Has anyone seen him?"

Jessica shook her head. "Nothing yet, but these volunteers are pretty dedicated. So far, we've covered the northern and northeastern parts of Milwaukee, and the surrounding suburbs. We won't quit until we find him." She sat down at the kitchen table. "A volunteer asked, has anyone tried to locate his phone yet? Or any other device that might have GPS, like a smart watch?"

Finn took out his phone. "My mom installed some sort of app on our phones to track us when we were teens. We got into a big argument about it, but none of us were really going to fight her. I never deleted it. I'm not sure if Con ever did either. Besides, can't his phone company do that?"

Jessica shook her head. "Sure, if we knew what phone company he uses. We don't even know what kind of phone he has. Not all phones can be tracked."

Finn pecked at his phone. "I no longer have the app my mom used." A frustrated expression crossed his face. "But it's been years. I imagine Con has at least upgraded his phone, maybe even given in to an iPhone. He held off long enough. Carried around this old Android flip phone when he was in the seminary. Said anything more was inappropriate."

John ran a hand through his hair. Con didn't have a materialistic bone in his body. He was more likely to give away any gift of new technology, including a new phone. He pointed at Dan. "Ask your mother about Con's phone. She would know what he carried, probably down to the last detail. They talked all the time. She was always worried about him. She didn't like the neighborhoods he hung out in."

Dan pulled his phone from a jacket pocket. "I know she's en route with Aunt Roz, but maybe I can catch her at the airport." He dialed and waited. "Phone went to voice mail." He dialed again. This time, he left a message. "Ma, it's Danny. We need to know about Con's phone. Call me back." He gazed at his father. "I guess we have to wait."

Jessica frowned. "We need the police involved. They can break through all the red tape." She closed her eyes and took a deep breath. "Is there anything else that might have GPS? A smart watch? Anything?"

Finn snapped his finger. "A St. Christopher medal. It has chip in it. I gave it to him as a birthday gift a few years ago."

Jessica's eyes rounded. "He still wears it. At least he was wearing it when I met him. Do you remember how it works?"

Finn scrolled through his phone. "God, I don't remember. I think it was affiliated with one of those *help, I've fallen, and can't get up* companies."

John snorted. "That's a big help." He gazed at Jessica. "Until my wife gets back to us, we've got nothing. I'm sorry. We should have come better prepared. I just thought the police would have our backs. I can't believe this seventy-two-hour rule." He gestured at the people working around him. "Put us to work. I feel like I'm going to explode. This is so damn frustrating."

Jessica went to her dining room table and picked up some paperwork. She handed it to him. "This is a list of all the medical clinics, urgent care centers, and hospitals in the southeastern counties. Call them, identify yourself, and tell them you are looking for your son. Ask by name, then ask about any John Does. Send them a copy of the flyer if they'll take it. I've loaded the poster on several computers, so it can be sent electronically." She motioned to a group across the room. "They'll help."

John studied the list. "Why aren't we contacting local police departments?"

Jessica shook her head. "We're trying to stay positive. We believe Con's been injured, and it's more likely he sought medical care. And until we can file a Missing Persons Report, the police won't help, anyway."

Finn continued to surf his phone. "Hopefully, I'll remember where I bought that medal if those calls get us nothing."

A hopeful expression crossed Dan's face. "Where did you buy the medal? If you don't remember, how did you pay for it?"

Finn's eyes grew wide, and he slapped his forehead. "Dammit, you're right. I don't remember how I paid for it, but I'm pretty sure it wasn't cash, because I had it mailed to him. I just need to search my bank account and my credit card records. I can even pinpoint the date, just not the year. It was a birthday present." He looked around the room. "Is there a spare computer I can use?"

Jessica motioned toward her laptop on the dining room table. "Use mine. I have a tablet I can work on." She crossed her hands over her heart. "Please, please, *please* let this be the answer." She offered Finn a shy smile. "I'm really glad you're here."

Dan snickered. "Hey, what about the rest of us?"

Jessica laughed. "Well, I know Syd will be glad to see you. And Con's father is always welcome.

"Now get to work."

"I've got it!" Finn threw up his hands and grinned.

"I bought that medal five years ago from a place called *Saints and Medals*. He reached for his phone and began dialing. When he connected, he rushed into an explanation of what he was looking for. His lips pursed, and he paused. "What do you mean you might no longer have the purchase on file?" He set the phone on speaker and the room quieted.

"It all depends on whether your brother or another family member continued to pay the tracking fee. Do you know if anyone has tried to track him since the purchase?"

Finn rolled his eyes. "I doubt anyone knew he could be tracked. Is there any way to see if the tracker was activated?"

"Only if the fee was paid."

Finn withheld a frustrated sigh. "Can you please check? I'd really appreciate it."

"Do you have the transaction ID? It should be on the receipt."

"But I don't have a receipt. It was five years ago."

The woman responded, but John rushed over and checked the computer screen. He interrupted. "We have the credit card transaction ID, and all the details of the purchase. Will that help?"

The woman audibly sighed. "Please provide the name, address, purchase date, amount, item details, credit card number, owner, and other order numbers of the recipient."

Finn's eyes widened. "We've got that. However, the address where it was sent is no longer where the recipient lives."

"Well, if he continued to pay the tracking fee, that shouldn't matter."

Finn nodded. "Okay, here's what we got." He read off the information on the screen.

"One moment, please."

The tension in the room seemed to swell as everyone waited.

The customer service employee returned. "Okay, one platinum St. Christopher Medal with a tracking chip sent to Reverend Connor J. O'Brien, St. Alphonsus Seminary, West Holt, Connecticut. The tracking was activated upon receipt until two thousand twenty."

Finn threw his pen across the room in frustration. "Dammit."

John held up his hand. "Is there any way to reactivate it? Maybe by paying any back fees and penalties?"

"Let me check, sir." The woman could be heard typing.

Then she paused. "Yes, it can be reactivated. However, there is no guarantee that the tracker is operational. If the medal has not been taken care of properly, the tracker may be dysfunctional or broken."

John's face reddened, and his jaw flexed, as if he was holding back his anger. In a very clipped voice, he responded, "If my son was wearing it, I can assure you he took very good care of it. Now let's see what's working and reactivate it. My son's life may depend on it."

Typing could be heard. "The reactivation fee of one hundred dollars, plus back fees of fifty dollars per year, will bring the total owed to three hundred dollars, plus tax."

Both Finn and John reached for their pockets and extracted a credit card. Finn gazed at his father. "Let me do this, Dad. It was a gift from me, and if it helps find Con, that's a gift returned ten times over."

John nodded. "Go ahead, son."

Finn provided the charge information. After it was confirmed, he asked, "How long before it will be activated?"

The representative paused. "Let's see here. Normally, reactivation takes seven to ten days. However, this is obviously an emergency. If you can get a warrant from a law enforcement agency, the turnaround will be within twenty-four hours. Would you like contact information to begin that process?"

Finn jumped to his feet and stalked across the room to Jessica, who had burst into tears. He side-hugged her and murmured into her ear. "It's okay. Let them throw up the roadblocks and choke us with red tape. O'Briens never back down and we never lose. We *will* get Con back."

He turned toward his father. He was carefully recording the information provided by the customer service representative. When the call ended, John nodded at Jessica. "Jess, this is your bailiwick. Who do you know who can get us this warrant?"

"Normally, I'd say the Milwaukee Police, but it might take a while. Over twenty-four hours, at least. However, one of my cousins is married to a small-town police chief nearby." She gestured toward John. "Let's go somewhere quiet, so I can make the call." She tugged at Finn's hand. "You, too."

Dan shot to his feet. "Don't leave me out, he's my brother, too."

Jessica led them to an empty bedroom and called her cousin Deb. After Jessica explained what they needed, Deb promised to contact her husband and get him to call her back.

Jessica collapsed on the bed and scowled. "I am so sick of these delays. Every minute that passes could make a difference in whether Con is found dead or alive. Why doesn't anyone understand that?"

Dan sat down and nudged her. "Thank a lawyer."

She stared at him. "What?"

"Why do you think everyone is making us jump through so many hoops? Lawsuits. No one wants to take a risk anymore, for fear they'll be sued. These days, you can find a lawyer to sue for anything, no matter how frivolous. Unless lawyers start better policing their own and stop all the bullshit lawsuits, people like us are going to suffer."

Jessica gazed at him and swiped at the new tears. "Dammit, you're right." She reached into her pocket and pulled out a rosary.

Daniel nudged her again. "Wow, it's been a long time since I've seen one of those."

John cleared his throat. "If more people prayed than sued, we'd have a far better world. Got another one of those?"

When Moira O'Brien swept into Jessica's house, she found her family praying, and it warmed her heart.

Prayers were what her son needed right now. By God's grace, Con would soon be found and returned to them. Moira had been taught the power of prayer by her granddad and had tried to pass that on to her children. With Con, she had succeeded. But now, seeing her sons and her dear husband in quiet contemplation, she was overwhelmed with joy. She knew the key to finding her son was prayer. God would provide.

Upon seeing her, John jumped to his feet and ran to his wife. He grabbed her and pressed her against him. "Moira, I am so glad you're here. I needed you."

Moira smiled up at him. "Did'ya now, my darling? And what is it you're needing?" Born in the County Cork, Moira had immigrated to the United States as a teen. Though a citizen for over thirty years, her Irish lilt still rose to the surface. However, her burnished red hair, unblemished ivory skin, and bright green eyes made her heritage clear. Even perfect English wouldn't alter that.

John nuzzled her, then pulled back, and his face turned stern. "Where have you been, and why haven't you responded to our calls?"

"Yeah, Ma. I left you a dozen messages." Dan pointed at the phone she pulled from her purse.

She flushed. 'Well, I turned it off at the airport and I guess I forgot to turn in back on." She glanced at it. "Oh, my. Forty-six messages." She paled. "What is going on?"

Dan grabbed her phone and examined it. He pushed a few buttons and smiled. "Bingo. Once a mother, always a mother."

Moira frowned. "What the devil are you going on about?"

Dan held up the phone to his father. "She still has the tracking app."

John chuckled. "Of course she does. She's had the same phone for years. She refuses to get a new one. The real question is, does she still use that app to spy on her sons?"

Moira slapped him on the arm. "I'm not spying. Sometimes I just check in to make sure it's working."

Finn pulled his mother in for a hug and kissed her cheek. "And is it still working, Ma? In particular, for Con?"

Moira's face lit up. "Yes, it does. I made sure of it. He's in and out of all these bad neighborhoods and he knows I worry. So, he agreed…" She gazed at Finn. "You think this will help us find Con?"

Finn nodded. "You could be our only hope."

Moira's eyes filled, her bottom lip trembled, and she nodded. A cheer went up in the room and she startled. Quickly, she grabbed the phone from Finn and fiddled with it. After a few seconds, she gazed at her husband and smiled. "This says he's at twenty-second and Rutherford. Where's that?" Without waiting for a reply, she tugged at John. "Let's go get our boy."

Jessica and several others in the room groaned.

John gazed at Jessica. "What? We've found Con. Why aren't you celebrating?"

Jessica made a face. "That's the inner city. A place where people shoot first, ask questions later. And with that white face and red hair, your wife's an instant target, as are any strangers who don't fit in. You head there, and you're just asking for it."

John's expression turned angry. "What do you expect us to do? Just sit here and wait until the police do their job?"

Jessica didn't respond. Instead, she took out her phone and swiped. "Syd? You anywhere near the inner city?"

"Well, we're on the Marquette Campus handing out flyers. Why?"

"According to the tracking app Con's mother has on her phone, Con—and or his phone—are at twenty-second and Rutherford."

"Oh, shit." Sydney paused. "Tell me you don't have me on speaker." Several people in the room chuckled. "Dammit, Jess. I told you to stop doing that. No one wants to hear my potty mouth."

Dan shouted, "I love your potty mouth, Syd."

Sydney tittered. "Among other things, Danny Boy."

Moira gasped, and Dan flushed.

Jessica just groaned. "Would you stop the flirting? You're already downtown. Can you head over there and check out the location?"

Sydney blew a raspberry into the phone. "Look, I may be an African queen, but there is no way this fine ebony face is heading into that neighborhood without a contingent of well-armed Marines. I don't dance on the wild side and I have no desire to start. This is a job for the police."

Jessica sighed. "Who won't do anything for…twelve more hours."

Someone said something to Sydney. A muted conversation ensued. "Hold on." More voices were heard. "Okay, we've got it covered. A guy with me knows someone who works in that precinct. He's going to ask him to do a drive-by, but he needs the map. Can you download it and send to me?"

Jessica raised her eyebrows. Her gaze swept the people gathered in her home. "Does anyone know how to do that?"

A petite woman of Asian origin raised her hand. "I think I can. Just get me the right email address."

"Sending to Jess's phone now."

Jessica's phone pinged. "Okay, Syd. We'll send the map to you."

"Roger that." Syd disconnected.

"Oh, for crying out loud, Moira, how long did you expect me to sit out in the car with all these groceries? Either the woman lets us use her kitchen or she doesn't. My lettuce is wilting and my potatoes are growing soft, and before long, this lamb is going to defrost and go bad. So stop petting that handsome lug of a husband and get to it. Can we use her kitchen or not?"

Jessica's mouth dropped open as another red-haired woman burst into her living room, armed with several grocery bags.

Finn rushed to her and relieved her of her packages. "Way to make an entrance, Aunt Roz." He smiled at Jessica. "What do you say? Can the O'Brien women cook while we wait? I think some Shepherd's Pie would really hit the spot about now."

Jessica gestured toward her kitchen. "Have at it. I'm starving."

Chapter Six: Miss Flora

Con wanted to scream.

She would not shut up. One minute she was talking, the next she was singing. How could anyone get any sleep around here? Wait. He was sleeping? Whew, that was a relief. For a while there, he thought he'd been cast into hell.

Still, that woman really should shut up. She was very annoying. Maybe he should just wake up and tell her. He tried to open an eye. Dammit. What did they do? Glue his eyelids shut? They weren't budging. Inwardly, he groaned. Maybe he should just... What the hell. Why couldn't he speak? Did they gag him as well? Okay, he needed to figure this out. Maybe he should listen.

"How's he doing?" A man spoke. A stranger. Con felt something cold brush his chest. The man harrumphed. "His heart rate has slowed, how's his blood pressure?"

"Down to one thirty over seventy, Doctor. It's stabilizing. Though there have been some spikes. I think he's having nightmares. He seems to be in great pain."

"Oxygen numbers okay? Any problem breathing?"

"That's been steady, Doctor."

"Well, let's keep everything as is, then. I don't want to increase the pain medication and put him further under than he is. I want to wake him up in the next couple of days."

Con sensed the doctor moving away from him.

"Maybe by then someone will have discovered he's missing and claim him. Poor schmuck. Someone certainly did a number on him. It would be nice to learn who he is finally."

The doctor's voice was further away. "Keep reading to him. Something simple. Not that kid wizard shit. Some of that scared the crap out of my kids. If he's already having nightmares, I don't want to make it worse. Stick to Dr. Seuss."

"What about music, Doctor?"

"If he's been having nightmares, no. His brain may distort sounds. Remember, coma mutes basic responses, so he can't tell you to shut it off. I don't want him going into A-Fib because music annoys him and he can't do anything about it."

Con heard a door shut quietly. He frowned. He barely comprehended any of that.

There was silence for a moment, then the nurse muttered, "A-hole. If you want to drive someone crazy read them children's books. Ask any parent." She patted Con's arm. "Don't you worry, honey, I have some romance novels that will scorch your crotch."

Con tried to smile. He wasn't sure what the woman was talking about, but it sounded good.

Pop! A stunning woman in a tight white gown slithered toward him. She tossed her blonde hair over a shoulder and pinned him with her Kewpie-like green eyes. In a sultry voice, she cooed, "Well, hello there, sailor." She moved beside him and hoisted her stilettoed foot onto a rock, revealing a shapely leg encased in a fishnet stocking. "Back to play?" She grinned seductively.

Con flushed. His entire body grew warm. A slim trail of sweat ran down his forehead.

The woman giggled. "Oh, baby, no need to be nervous." She chuckled, and the stealthy tongue of a snake flicked through her lips. She moved toward him and ran a hand down his chest. "You're so delicious, I just have to have you for dinner." The woman grabbed his neck and pulled him toward her.

Con screamed, frantically struggling. Suddenly, a burst of

strength enveloped him and he tossed the woman aside.

She collapsed onto the floor and glared at him. "How dare you." Her mouth opened wider to reveal dripping fangs. "I'm your wife. We were married at the altar of the devil. You submitted *to me*." She hissed. "There's no going back now, my husband. You rejected God to join me in Hell and the Devil told you then there's no going back." She flashed an evil grin, her red eyes filled with menace. "You are mine..." She crawled toward him.

Pop! "For goodness' sake, Connor. Why would you leave the seminary?" His mother shook her head. "What are we going to do with you?"

Pop! "Mr. O'Brien, you've been quite disruptive in class. Some might say you're rather dismissive of the rule of law. If you can't support the U.S. Constitution, how the hell can you practice law?"

Con shifted uncomfortably in his chair. "Sir, I plan to practice law for one reason and one reason only. I firmly believe in *truth, justice, and the American way*. And when the law prevents that, you'd better believe that me and my friend, Ben Franklin, are going to fight."

Pop! The elderly man gently placed a quill on his desk and sighed. He smiled kindly at Con. "My boy, I'm afraid you've really riled up those redcoats this time. Whatever did you hope to achieve by dumping all that tea in the harbor?"

Pop! The women kneeled at the altar. The sun shining through the stained-glass windows cast a spectrum of color around her. Wings bloomed from her shoulders and suddenly she levitated, her wings beating furiously. Her head turned, and she smiled gently at Con.

"I waited for you, Connor. I waited and waited and you didn't come back." She sobbed, and a tear dropped from her eye. "I love you, Con. Oh, why don't you love me back?"

Con moved toward her, his arms outstretched. "I'm trying

to come back to you, Jess. I'm really trying, but they won't let me."

She levitated further, escaping his grasp. "I promise you, wherever you go, I'll find you." Slowly, she drifted away.

Pop! A man with long, unruly hair and an overgrown five o'clock shadow strummed a chord on an electric guitar. He smirked. "Whattyathink, man? Love stinks, or maybe it hurts and sometimes it blows, but what the hell? No one turns down a wet, quivering..."

Pop! Con's world went black.

Officer Kent Long and his partner, Deandre Washington, pulled up to the curb and surveyed the homes at Twenty-second and Rutherford.

"Shit, this will be one of those needle-in-a-haystack searches." Long scratched his forehead. "Too many houses, too many people. Has that map shown up yet? We need to narrow it down. I don't want to knock on doors, riling up the neighborhood."

Washington chuckled. "Trying to avoid getting shot in that fine white ass?"

Long shrugged. "People aren't afraid of cops anymore. Too many have faced guns lately. I don't want to be one of them. I want to get in and out before any shooters notice."

Washington harrumphed. "Check out that blue house there." He pointed. "See that old lady in the window? She's the neighborhood watchdog. The minute we move, she's going to be on the phone with her neighbors, telling them to hide their guns and hide their sons. Any cop in the neighborhood makes them nervous, no matter the color. That's why the captain always tells us to act with precision. And then get the hell out."

Long's phone beeped. He peered at it. "Okay. According

to this, that old lady has a reason to keep her eyes on us. If this map is accurate, the phone is in her house."

Washington put on his uniform hat and adjusted his bulletproof vest. "Do we call it in?"

"Hell, yeah. I want back-up if this goes haywire."

"But the Captain didn't authorize it."

"I've got that covered. I reported the call to dispatch, said we were gonna check it out. If things get nasty, we get out and wait for backup."

Washington sighed. He clasped the St. Christopher medal he wore around his neck—a gift from his wife—and gazed heavenward.

Long smirked at the man's short prayer. He had long ago stopped believing in God. He had seen too much. No God of his would allow anyone to live in these neighborhoods. Bullets coming through the walls at all hours, some hitting kids. The horrendous squalor—mold, insects, rats, lead pipes. This was America, dammit. A country that should be capable of taking care of their own. He touched his gun and said softly, "Let's hit it."

Together, the men exited the patrol car and headed up to the house. Before they reached the porch, a car swept up to the curb, its brakes screeching. Instinctively, the two men whipped around, their hands reaching for their guns.

A large man, his white clerical collar offset by a dark face, got out of the car, his hands thrust above his head. "Calm down, gentleman. I didn't mean to startle you. When Miss Flora calls and tells me she's about to be arrested, I get my butt in my car and hustle."

'Well, hell's bells, Reverend, we haven't even pushed her doorbell." Washington glared at the preacher. "How the hell did she know what we wanted? We haven't even spoken to her."

Long kept his hand on his weapon. "Unless she knows why

we're here and is gonna hide behind your robes."

The reverend stopped and pointed at Long. "Now, you see there? That shitty attitude will get you nowhere. Innocent until proven guilty, though I can hardly wait to hear what crime you're wanting to charge an eighty-year-old woman with." He shook his head. "Shameful."

Long pulled out his phone and gestured to the man. "Allow me to show you, sir." Long pointed to the map on his screen. "A man has gone missing, and the family tracked his phone to this address. So, either the guy is in her home or somehow, she took possession of his phone. The blinking icon tells me the phone is currently in use."

The reverend frowned. "May I ask who's missing?"

Long hesitated, so Washington spoke. "That street lawyer guy. The one they call Saint Con."

"Connor O'Brien? When did this happen? I haven't heard anything."

Long shrugged. "Above my pay grade, I believe. I just found out when his phone was tracked."

The preacher grasped Long's shoulder. "Connor is well-known in these parts. Let's find out what Miss Flora knows." He stepped onto the well-worn porch and knocked on the door. "Miss Flora, it's Reverend Bingham. Can we speak?"

The door opened slowly, and an elderly woman, her white hair shooting from her scalp in wire-like spirals, peered at the people at the door. She pushed up her glasses and sniffed. "Good gracious, Pastor, I'm not fit for company. I haven't even put my wig on yet."

The minister smiled, his deep brown eyes regarding her with amusement. "This isn't a social call, Miss Flora, so there's no need to spiff up that beautiful face. These men have a few questions for you, and they're important."

Miss Flora screwed up her face. "About what? I ain't done nothing."

Rev. Bingham snorted. "When a retired schoolteacher slips into black speak, you can't help but believe she's guilty of something."

Washington gazed at the woman. "Please, ma'am, a man's life may be at stake."

"What man.? Is it someone I know?" She avoided looking the officer in the eye.

"Connor O'Brien, ma'am. They call him Saint Con. The lawyer with the food truck." Long fumbled with his phone and brought up a photo of Connor. "This man? Do you know him?"

Miss Flora's expression softened. "Con is missing?" She slapped a hand over her mouth and her eyes widened in horror, but she said nothing.

The minister stiffened, but inquired gently, "Miss Flora, his phone was tracked to your home. Now, why would you have his phone?"

The old woman emitted a sad sigh, and her eyes filled with tears. "Googly gave it to me. Said Mr. Speaks found it somewhere and told him to pass it on to me." Her face crumbled. "Tell me Googly did nothing wrong. I've worked so hard to keep him out of trouble."

"Miss Flora, you go get that phone. Let me talk to these officers." When she disappeared from sight, Rev. Bingham cleared his throat and shook his head. "Googly's a good kid. Miss Flora's been raising him since his parents took off. It's just that some neighbors aren't as God-fearing or upstanding as she. Poor Googly's between a rock and a hard place. He's trying to fit in, but it's not so easy. And Speaks is the father of those two boys who are being held for that shooting on the East Side. That family is trouble, a blight on this neighborhood. How the heck did they get his phone?"

Washington sighed. "Maybe they're the reason he's missing. We need to get that phone and call this in. Screw the seventy-two-hour waiting period. This smells bad, really bad."

Long nodded. "Amen."

Chapter Seven: The Phone

Dr. Wood adjusted the IV drip and turned to the nurse assisting him.

"Now that his vitals have stabilized, we need to bring him out of the coma slowly. I wrote down the schedule for reducing his intake of sedatives. Follow it closely." He handed the nurse her notepad. After she left, he stood by the Con's bedside and muttered. "Who are you? Why is no one looking for you?"

A low humming sound distracted him. His gaze swept the room. Where was that noise coming from? A machine keeping this man alive...was it malfunctioning? Quickly, he pressed the call button and when a nurse responded, he said, "Get a tech in here. I don't need a patient dying on me because a machine supposed to be keeping him alive goes belly up."

He muttered, "I had enough of that shit during COVID." He heard the humming sound again. It had to be coming from a machine. It was too close to the bed. A tech rushed into the room, toolbox in hand. Dr. Wood pointed to the machine hooked up to the patient. "Something is emitting a low humming noise. Like a battery or motor is running out."

The tech stopped and listened. His face screwed up in concentration. Quickly, he checked all the monitors and shrugged. "I don't know what it could be. I don't hear any humming noise and all the screens are operating correctly." He bent down and checked the outlet. "Everything is plugged in. Nothing here operates on a battery, unless the power goes out." His expression was skeptical, but Dr. Wood knew the tech wouldn't be dumb enough to question his hearing.

"Look, all I know is I heard something humming. A noise is being made, perhaps from a machine or impact on it. We can't take that chance."

The tech dropped to his knees and checked under the bed. When he got back on his feet, he offered a wry smile. "Well, at least we know there's not a bomb under his bed."

The doctor rolled his eyes. Then he heard it again. *Hmmmmm.* "There. That's the noise I'm talking about."

The tech looked around the room. "It almost sounds like one of those watch alarms. Was the guy wearing one when he was brought in?"

The doctor crossed the room to the closet where a patient's personal effects were normally stored. It was empty. The Sheriff had probably taken the clothing for evidence. *Hmmmmm.*

The tech spun around, trying to source the noise. Finally, he opened a bedside cabinet and pulled out a small plastic bag. "A rosary and a St. Christopher's medal. I'm guessing one of these has a tracking chip."

Dr. Wood smiled widely. "Which means someone is looking for this guy. And we're going to help them find him."

Sadie English hoisted the box of sample bagel sandwiches and grunted.

"Geesh, Dad. How many sandwiches are there in here? Are you trying to feed the entire city of Burlington?"

Jeb English laughed. "When I first opened this shop, I gave out hundreds of sandwiches. In our business, it's not enough to run ads that claim our food is good. We have to prove it. Otherwise, we'll wind up with negative reviews on Yelp, and that would kill your mother."

"Well, okay, but why would someone who lives or works in Burlington travel all the way to the south side of

Milwaukee to buy a sandwich? That's at least a forty-five-minute drive. And I know there are sandwich shops in Burlington. That's like me driving all the way to Kenosha just to buy a Cyclops."

"Ah, but what if, after tasting one of our delicious creations, you learn they're being sold in downtown Burlington and we deliver?"

Sadie shot her father a stink-eye. "You're opening a new shop and you didn't tell me?"

Jeb rolled his eyes. "Sadie, your mother and I have been talking about it right in front of you for weeks. You've been off in coo-coo land. Your head is so far up your..." He blushed. "Well, you know what I mean. You're so wrapped up in everyone else's business, you don't have time for your own."

Sadie planted her fists on her hips. "Seriously, Dad? I think I would have paid attention if you'd mentioned it." Her eyes narrowed. "Who's running the new shop? And why wasn't I asked?"

"Actually, I didn't think you'd want to move to Burlington. Given that bakers arrive at four in the morning and sales staff and cooks at six, you'd soon grow tired of the drive. Besides, we'll be operating out of a coffee shop down there at first. We'll deliver fresh bagels and sandwiches each morning. This is merely a test run to see if our sandwiches will sell." He turned and placed a stack of paper on the sample box. "I've given you a list of businesses, but make sure you hit the hospital first. They're always hungry. And make sure you leave lots of Saint Con flyers. I can't believe he hasn't been found yet. I finally got ahold of some of that Fair Trade coffee he's always razzing me about." Jeb sighed. "I keep thinking he might never taste it. Hell, as it is, he may be the only person who will drink it. It's going to cost a quarter more than our other drinks."

Sadie sighed. She knew the longer Connor O'Brien was missing, the more likely it was that he was dead. And for her friend Jess, that sucked eggs. She had finally shown some interest in a man, and before the romance got off the ground, the guy disappeared. Some say when you make plans, God laughs, but this was not funny. She screwed her face up in disgust. When she hit those pearly gates, she and God were going to have a sit-down, and she was going to raise heck about all the non-funny moments in her life.

Her father interrupted her thoughts. "Oh, I almost forgot." He pulled out an envelope. "Hand out these cards, too. Anyone who completes our online survey will receive a special code they can use for twenty-five percent off their first order. Make sure everyone gets one."

Sadie saluted. "Aye, aye, almighty chief." She shoved the cards into her purse, hoisted the box, and turned toward the front door, singing, *Hi-ho, hi-ho, off to work I go…"*

John O'Brien shut down his phone and dropped his head into hands.

God, it had been an awful day. He was going crazy with worry for his son. Everywhere they turned, there was a roadblock. And now there was another. A soft hand stroked his cheek.

"Who was it, John? Is there news about Connor?" Moira gazed at her husband, her eyes filled with concern. The soft lilt of Ireland was even stronger in her voice, a sure sign that she shared his exhaustion. "Have they found something?"

John wiped his eyes, surprised at the moisture he found there. He might be a tough guy on Wall Street, but when it involved his family, he turned to mush. How could this be happening? And to Con? People called him *saint* in jest, but in John's mind, Connor was closer to God than anyone he knew. "That was the company that sold the St. Christopher medal to Finn. They turned on the tracker, but they could not pick up a location. Apparently, they use satellites to triangulate, but there are a lot of things that could block the signal. Buildings, vehicles, elevators, lead in walls, the like. If Con isn't out in the open or near an open window, the tracker probably won't work. It would give off a buzzing noise, but that's only helpful if someone else hears it."

Several phones went off in the room, and hope struck John's heart. He stared at Jessica as she spoke to someone. Finally, she disconnected. Jessica bit her lip, as if trying to decide what to say.

"What is it?" Moira moved over to Jessica and took her hand.

Jessica took a deep breath and gazed at her. She held up her hand and said loudly, "Hey, guys, listen up. There's news." The room quieted. "The Milwaukee Police Department has announced they are launching an investigation into Con's disappearance. It will be on all TV news stations and social media within the hour." Everyone cheered, but Jessica again held up her hand.

Before she could say anything more, Dan ran into the room and shouted, "They found Con's phone!" He started jumping around in excitement.

Jessica glared at him and snapped, "Would you let me finish?"

Dan's mouth dropped open to protest, but his father made a zipping motion across his mouth, then nodded at Jessica. "Please, continue. They found his phone…"

"But they haven't found Con yet. The father of the kids involved in the convenience store shooting gave it to a woman who lived in their neighborhood, and it was tracked there. The officers who found it went to the father's home and questioned him. The man wouldn't let them into the house, but through an open door they spotted a dog chewing on a wallet that looked like it was covered in blood. When questioned about it, the man bolted."

Jessica swiped at a curl that had fallen into her eye. "Long story short, the wallet belonged to Con. The man has been brought in for questioning."

Moira asked hesitantly. "Did they search the house?"

Jessica nodded. "That's all they found. The man said his dog found the wallet, but the police know Con was beaten by the man's sons and disappeared. They're checking all the traffic cams to see if they can determine what really happened."

Finn frowned. "Why didn't she answer the phone when we called?"

Jessica shrugged. "She suspected the phone was stolen and didn't want to bring the police to her door. She only used it for outgoing calls."

John gazed at her. "So the good news is that the police are now involved. The bad news is we still don't know where Con is or even…" He struggled to maintain his composure. "Even if he's alive."

Moira emitted a soft sob. "He is, John. In my heart, I feel it. God has always protected Con, and he's protecting him now." She gazed at Jessica. "So, again, we wait?"

"Not a chance. We keep looking. And pray the father breaks and tells us what really happened. He knows something."

Sydney pulled her car to the curb and killed the ignition.

She gazed at the volunteer accompanying her and said, "Get behind the wheel and wait. If old Squeezer tries to bolt, chase him down. I'll go after him on foot." She pulled her purse off the floor and extracted two ten-dollar bills. "A little cash never hurts with these guys."

The volunteer's eyes widened. "Maybe we should call the cops."

Sydney huffed. "That'll send Squeezer into the 'burbs, and we'll never find him. We need to find Con. The clock is ticking. Squeezer was there that day. He saw something." She slid out of her car and headed to a group trying to drum up money by washing the windshields of drivers stopped at the traffic lights. The problem was, the men didn't ask if the motorists wanted their windshields cleaned. They just did it and then demanded money.

She spotted Squeezer dipping a cloth in a bucket and sauntered over to him. "Hey, Squeezer, got a minute?"

Squeezer lifted his pale blue eyes and glared at Sydney. "You a cop?" He shifted from foot to foot, prepared to flee.

Sydney stuck a pose and waved her hand down her body. "Now, why would you think I'd spoil this delicious body with that ugly uniform?" She flashed a ten-dollar bill and winked. "I'm just interested in a conversation."

Squeezer tugged at his dirty gray hair and studied her. "About what?"

Sydney nodded to a spot up on the curb not currently occupied. "Let's chat over there. I imagine you don't want your friends to think you're buying them dinner with your potential windfall." She strode across the street.

Squeezer looked up and down the street, then followed. "Hey, lady. What's this all about?"

Sydney turned and blocked Squeezer from the view of the other Squeegee guys. She placed a ten-dollar bill in his hand. "That's my show of goodwill. You'll get another if you tell me what I want to hear." Sydney reached into her pocket and turned on her phone recorder.

Squeezer smirked. "Which is?"

"Saint Con. Monday you saw Saint Con get roughed up by a couple of kids. In his truck. Then the kids ran away. I need to know what happened to Con." When Squeezer hesitated, Sydney glared at him. "Look, I know you were there. You took the guy's donuts." She flashed the second ten-dollar bill. "What happened after those boys ran?"

Squeezer shrugged. "Some big black guy pulled up and said he'd take care of 'im. I helped 'im move the Saint to a van. Guy said he would take him to the hospital. He gave me a fiver and told me to forget his face. I tried to tell a cop that, but he laughed at me." He suddenly looked uncomfortable. "Why? I assumed the guy *was* taking Saint to a doctor or a hospital. He was in bad shape."

Sydney shook her head. "Well, he didn't. Not around here, anyway. Tell me about the van. Dark? Light? Any writing on the side?"

Squeezer scratched his head. "Dark, maybe blue? I don't 'member any writing, but he had funny plates, like from another state. White with some light blue, I think."

Sydney withheld a groan. Almost every surrounding state had some version of a blue on white plate. "Tell me about the guy. Was he wearing a uniform, or just regular clothes?"

Squeezer broke into a smile, revealing dirty teeth. "Yeah, he was dressed like a bus driver."

"Remember a badge or something around his neck?"

Squeezer shook his head. "Naw, but when we were moving Saint, I saw a tattoo around his wrist. It was an eagle sitting on a cowpie or something. Pretty funny. And another thing, the guy was big, dark, and ugly. Mean like. If I wasn't helping Saint, I'd of run the other way."

Sydney handed him another ten-dollar bill. "Where can I find you if I have more money to spend?"

Squeezer grinned again. "Same alley, five garages up. Old lady Swanson lets me sleep on an old bed in her garage. Said I keep out the *hobos*." He rolled his eyes. "Funny, I thought I was one."

Sydney flashed him a brilliant smile. "Naw, you've got more class than that. Besides, you may have saved Saint's life. And if you did, that makes you a hero."

Squeezer puffed out his chest and crowed, "A hero, huh? I think my mother would have liked that."

Sydney lightly punched his arm. "Thanks, honey. Don't spend all that money on booze, okay?"

"Oh, hell no. I'm going to go have lunch with the King."

Sydney grinned. "I'd join you, but time's a wasting. I need to find Saint before it's too late." She waved and headed back to her car, where she ducked into the front passenger seat and smiled at the volunteer. "Start driving, I have to make a call. I have proof that Con was taken. Now we need to figure out where."

Chapter Eight: No Longer John Doe

Jessica could not control her nerves. They were getting closer. She could feel it. But would they find Con in time?

She closed her eyes and prayed silently. *Please God, keep Con safe until we find him.* A feeling of peace washed over her, and Jessica smiled. Con had been missing for three days now and she was exhausted, but her need to find the man who had touched her heart squelched that. She couldn't sleep. Not until Con was found. Thankfully, Con's mother and aunt were keeping her well-fed. At least her stomach was full. Her brain, however, was on overload. Any more coffee and her mind would be pickled.

Jessica tried to assess the information they had gathered so far. Sydney's confirmation that Con had been taken from his truck had spurred the police to scour area traffic cams and security cameras. They quickly established that Isiah and Moses Speaks had, in fact, attacked Con. Upon sighting some gang rivals up the street, they'd left Con hurt and bleeding. However, before they fled, they could be seen searching his pockets, taking his phone and wallet.

Jessica could not shake off the guilt she was feeling. While she was throwing a pity-party for being stood up, Con had been fighting for his life.

Con must have been horribly confused when Donovan Speaks, the father of the two shooters, appeared in the alley and moved Con to his van. Thankfully, a nearby business caught Speaks' arrival with their alley cam. Although the video was of poor quality, the police could clearly identify the elder Speaks, as well as Squeezer.

The police technicians tracked Speaks and his van to a southbound state highway. However, that was where the trail ended. When the police finally found Speaks hiding in a shed in an adjacent neighborhood and brought him in for questioning, he refused to provide further information. After the police revealed the video of Speaks taking Con from his truck, the man finally broke down.

He told the police that he had been late to pick up his teenage sons from the East Side. When he got there, he saw them running from Con's truck, so he stopped to investigate. When he found Con bloody and beaten, he assumed his sons, ages fourteen and fifteen, were facing potential murder charges, possibly as adults. Lesser crimes resulted in time in juvenile detention, but the local courts routinely moved teen murder suspects into adult court. If found guilty, his boys could face many years in an adult prison. Speaks had done his stint in jail. He knew what happened to kids when thrown in with adults. It wasn't pretty.

So, to protect his sons, Speaks removed Con from the scene. He told the police he was unaware his sons were involved in an altercation up the street until he heard gunshots. At that point, the need to hide Con intensified, so he fled. While he admitted to dumping Con's body in a cornfield, he swore he was alive then. However, he could not recall where the dumping occurred. Just somewhere *south of the city*. How could he not remember where?

Jessica felt like she had been yanked into an alternate reality. Nothing made sense. This did not happen to normal people. Why hadn't Con been found? The police were searching all the areas south, from Racine County to the state line. Although Con's photo had been widely distributed, volunteers were focusing on all area medical facilities. They were also checking with rural police departments, and homeless shelters or soup kitchens.

Moira came out of the kitchen with a plate filled with the ingredients of an Irish breakfast. It included bacon, sausages, fried eggs, baked beans, sauteed mushrooms, fried tomatoes, and hash browns. Thankfully, no blood pudding was included. Moira slid the plate in front of Jessica. "You need to soak up some of that coffee you've been shoveling into your stomach or you're going to crash from the caffeine overload." She placed a fork and napkin next to the plate.

The food cast out delicious scents, pulling Jessica from her negative thoughts. She nodded. "When we find Con, I swear I'll sleep for a week. I won't get out of bed until my stomach is screaming for food."

Moira frowned. "I don't know you well, but my sons tell me Con is quite fond of you. What if he needs you once we find him? You'll be no good to him if you collapse from exhaustion. Eat, then you go take a nap. I'll wake you if there's any news, and I'll ask another volunteer to monitor your phone."

"What about you, Moira? Your family hasn't slept either. We are all so fatigued, I imagine once Con is found, we'll all collapse."

Moira offered a slight smile. "True enough, but the alternative—not finding my Connor—is unacceptable. As long as there is hope, I will not give up. I simply can't." She nodded at her husband, who was sound asleep in a recliner. "I'll try to rest when John wakes. When a mother's child is in peril..." She shrugged, then squeezed Jessica's shoulder. "Eat, then rest. While you can."

At that moment, Jessica's phone rang. Suddenly, all eyes were on her. She grabbed her cell phone and glanced at Moira's face. She shook her head. "Relax, it's just Sadie. She probably just wants an update." She swiped at her phone. "Hey, we have nothing yet. The police are still searching."

"Jess, I found Connor!" she screamed into the phone. "He's here, and he's alive." She shrieked. "I dropped off some sandwiches, and I heard some nurses talking about a John Doe, so I showed them the flyer. They took it to some doctor who said he thought it was Saint Con. A farmer found him in his fields and the EMTs brought him in." Sadie sobbed. "Oh, Jess, he's alive. He's alive!"

Jessica fought to hang onto her phone as the tears flowed. She couldn't speak.

John rose from his chair and sleepily took the phone from her. Sadie had been so loud that everyone heard her announcement. "Where is my son?" He, too, appeared overwhelmed. His eyes were glassy, as if he was about to shed tears.

Jessica took the phone from him and turned on the speaker. Sadie spoke, but Jessica interrupted her. Sadie was one of those people who leaped before she looked, often reaching conclusions without having all the facts. "Sadie, are you absolutely sure it's Con?"

Sadie was quiet for a moment. "Well, his face is heavily bandaged, and he's just now coming out of a coma..."

Moira gasped and wrung her hands, whispering, "Oh, dear."

"Sadie." Jessica's voice was tired, but stern. "How do you know it's Con?"

"His tattoos. He has an angel on his right shoulder, a devil on the left, and a Celtic cross on his arm, though it's pretty messed up. And he has dark hair, and the doctor says his eyes are blue. This guy is also pretty buff, like Con." Sadie paused. "Oh, and the doctor says he has a St. Christopher medal that keeps buzzing. He tried to track down the company that made it but got nowhere. He says the darn thing just keeps buzzing." Sadie giggled with excitement. "I know it's him, Jess."

Jessica tried to hide her skepticism. "Okay, where are you?"

"Burlington Memorial Hospital."

Jessica frowned. She turned to Con's parents. "That's about forty-five minutes away."

Sadie shouted, "Jess, pay attention. He's here, and he's alive. Get your butt in a car and get on Highway Thirty-Six and get here. They had Con in a medically induced coma, but they're bringing him out of it. The doctor says he's going to wake up soon." Sadie sighed dramatically. "Wouldn't it be wonderful if the first thing he sees when he wakes up is his lady love?"

John harrumphed and swiped at his cheeks.

Everyone in the room was in tears. The past few days had been tense. All the volunteers were exhausted. Moira and Aunt Roz had kept the volunteers fed, but right now, sleep was what they needed.

Sadie spoke to someone, then yelled, "Get your ass down here, girlfriend!"

Knowing Sadie's tendency to jump the gun, Jessica again asked, "Sadie, are you absolutely sure it's Con? You have absolutely no doubt?"

"Unless Con has a twin or a clone, I am absolutely sure we have found him."

Moira moaned and crossed herself. She murmured, "Thank the Lord. My son is alive." She went to her husband and embraced him.

Jessica stared at everyone, her expression one of puzzlement. "We've found Con, people. Why is everyone crying?" She absently swiped at her own cheeks.

Moira tried to smile. "Tears of joy, my darling. Tears of joy."

Jessica and Con's family piled into her neighbor's SUV. They were all coasting on fumes and none of them was fit to drive. Thankfully, James DeWitt had insisted on ferrying them to the hospital.

"My GPS says we will be there in about forty-five minutes," he said. "Do I need to stop for coffee or anything else before I get on the highway? If memory serves me, there's a drive-thru right before the entrance ramp."

Moira vehemently shook her head. "No, I just want to get there and hug my son. Too bad this car doesn't have wings."

Finn smirked. "Best get to it. We know better than to argue with Ma. We can get food when we get to the hospital, *after* we see Con."

"If it really is Con," Jessica muttered. Sadie had made dramatic claims before only to fall flat on her face. She was more about the drama than the facts. "Sadie has been wrong before. She means well, but sometimes, she jumps the gun." She gazed at the O'Briens. "I want to believe she found him, but if it isn't Con, I'm going to be crushed, and I am sure you will be as well."

Moira grasped her hand. "I choose to have faith. And if it isn't Con, we'll just keep on looking. I will not give up on my son."

Tears filled Jessica's eyes again as she recalled her last conversation with Con. Their conversation had been playful, filled with anticipation over their lunch date.

Con had ended the call with, *I'll have you know, doll, that I'm not fooling around here. I'm too old for that. I know what I want, and I mean to get it. And what I want is you.* Did he still feel that way? Would he even remember her? The uncertainty was killing her. Their promising start could very well have an empty ending. Jessica could not avoid voicing her greatest fear. "What if he doesn't know us? What if he has amnesia or, worse, brain damage?"

John shot her a fierce look. "Let's not invite trouble. We won't know anything until Con awakes. And if he doesn't remember us at first, we'll help him remember. And if there's brain damage, we'll get him the help and give him the support he needs. That's what families do."

Dan sighed. "You realize if that is Con lying in that hospital, they won't allow us to take him home, at least right away. We're going to have to stick around until he heals."

Jessica gulped. She had never considered that Con's family might want to take him home. Back to New York. Her disappointment soured her stomach. Her relationship with Con had barely begun. He made her feel things she had never experienced before. Taking him from her just wasn't fair. "I can help you find more long-term accommodations. At least something more comfortable than an extended stay hotel." She offered a slight smile.

Moira patted her arm. "We're fine for now. I imagine we can move into Con's house once he's out of the woods. I just didn't want to move in without his permission. My son is very protective of his privacy. He may not want us bothering him as he recovers."

John emitted a short laugh. "My wife is right. But I run a business. My employees are competent, but an extended absence could very well mess things up. Once we're confident he's recovering, me and my sons will have to get back to New York." He gazed at Moira. "I imagine that will leave you and Roz to manage things for a while." He smiled. "With the help of his friends, of course."

Moira sighed. "Which means the minute he's released, Con will put us on the next plane home. He gets testy when others hover."

John smiled at Jessica. "If he's as enamored of you as my sons claim, I imagine the only caregiver he's going to want is you."

Jessica blushed and shook her head. "Even I'd want my mother if something like this happened." She smiled at Moira. "I won't let him send you home until you're ready to leave."

Moira's fair skin pinked. "Thanks, but I don't want to be that kind of mother-in-law. I'll leave when Con asks me to leave."

Dan snickered. "After you install a baby com so you can watch his every move."

Moira leaned forward and cuffed the back of his head. "Quit while you're ahead, kid."

"Here it is," James announced as he pulled up to the front door of the hospital. "Do you want me to wait?

John shook his head. "Thanks, but I'm not sure how long we'll be inside. We'll make arrangements once we figure out…"

Jessica held up her hand, interrupting him. "Maybe we should make sure it is Con before we let Mr. DeWitt leave."

"Good idea," James said. "I'll park and wait in the lobby. Maybe one of you can come down and tell me what's what once you verify if it is or isn't Connor?"

Jessica smiled at him. "Thanks so much for the ride. You truly are the best neighbor. When we know something, I'll update you." She opened the car door. "Shall we?"

The minute they walked into the hospital lobby, Sadie barreled into her, screeching at the top of her lungs, "I can't believe it. I found Connor O'Brien." She threw her arms around Jessica. "He's not awake yet, but he will be soon." A single tear dropped from her eye. 'You can tell Syd that means I get to be maid of honor. Not her hoity toity ass."

Jessica attempted a smile. "Sure, Sadie. Whatever you want." She grabbed her hand. "Take us to him, please."

Sadie pulled her toward the elevator. "Come on. Dr. Wood, who has been taking care of him, is waiting."

Silently, Jessica and Con's family followed Sadie into the elevator and up to the eleventh floor. When the door opened, Sadie urged them forward. "Come on, he's in here." She led them into a room with two beds. One contained an elderly man, picking at his lunch. Sadie waved. "Hey, Henry, this is Con's family. I'm afraid it won't be so quiet anymore."

Henry nodded. "Good, it's been too quiet around here. Besides, a man needs his family sometimes." He saluted Sadie with a spoon. "Hope that means you'll still visit."

Sadie blew him a kiss. "Of course, you sweet man." She led the family around a curtain. A man lay in the hospital bed, unmoving. His head was swathed in bandages, and one arm was in a cast. A leg seemed to be twisted awkwardly under a thin blanket.

As Sadie pushed the curtain open, Dr. Wood was bent over his patient, checking his heart. He straightened upon seeing the family and a smile creased his face. His relief was obvious. He motioned to John and Moira. "Please, come forward. Tell me if this is your son."

John placed his arm protectively around Moira's shoulder. They stood there silently, as if assessing the man's injuries. Moira buried her head in her husband's chest and sobbed. "Look what they did to him. My Lord. He was beaten so badly. I cannot believe it."

John nodded at Dr. Wood. "It's Connor, my son. What the hell happened here?"

Dr. Wood sighed. "We can talk about that later. Right now, I think it's important he wakes up to people who love him. Cases like this can be dicey. He's been suspended somewhere between life and death, and even after the medication wears off, he may not come back fully for a while. Comas are brutal on patients' minds. Maybe his brain is reliving the worst times of his life, with his fear or anger or grief magnified exponentially. Or, remembering moments of extreme happiness, but the memories may be slightly distorted and end in tragedy. Maybe he is reliving his favorite cartoons. No one really knows and most coma victims don't remember. We know he has to decide on his own to live, to come back rather than merely escape the darkness. Talk to him, sing to him, read to him. Let the sound of your voices pull him back from the abyss." Dr. Wood shook his head. "Everything you say and do could make a difference."

Moira pulled away from John and leaned over Con, her hand grasping his. She kissed his forehead and murmured, "Come back to us, my sweet boy. You gave us quite a scare, but I haven't been this happy to see you since you left the priesthood. We've met your gurl, Jess. She's quite a beauty. Perfect for you. I love you, Connor O'Brien. Wake up so I can see your bonny smile." She turned to Jessica and held out her hand. "Come here, Jess. If anyone is going to wake this boy up, it's you."

Jessica blushed and stepped forward. She hadn't known Connor long enough to feel secure in their relationship. What if she was mistaking Connor's charm for affection? What if everyone else was overestimating his feelings for her? She could do more harm than good.

John pulled a chair over and motioned for her to sit down. "Why don't you two get reacquainted while we speak to the doctor?"

He and his family left the room. Sadie walked across the room to chat with Henry.

Jessica took Con's hand and brushed his black curls off his forehead. "This is a hell of a way to avoid a date, Connor O'Brien. When you didn't show up, I was pissed. Really pissed. I swore I'd never speak to you again. Then Syd told me you were missing and my heart broke into a thousand pieces. I don't know where we're headed, but I'd like to find out. So, open those gorgeous blue eyes of yours and let's get started." She leaned forward to kiss him, then pulled back in dismay. An oxygen mask covered his mouth. Sighing with resignation, she kissed his cheek.

Con's finger moved ever so slightly, then he moaned. Jess looked around wildly, knowing she should tell someone. Finally, she yelled, "Sadie, get the doctor, I think Con's waking up."

One of Connor's deep blue eyes popped open, and she gasped. "Con?" She waited.

Con groaned again, then both eyes popped over. He grinned at Jessica and said haltingly, "If this is heaven, I'm sticking around."

Jessica laughed and hugged him.

Con made a strangled noise. "Um, ouch?" he murmured.

Jessica jumped back. "Sorry, I forgot you must hurt all over."

Even though Con's face was heavily bandaged, he was obviously in pain. "W-a-ter?"

Jessica grabbed a paper cup with a straw off of a nearby table and stared at it in confusion. How was Con supposed to drink from this? Unfortunately, when she turned back to Con, his eyes were closed. He had fallen back asleep.

Relief filled her when Dr. Wood and Con's family rushed in. "He asked for water, but I didn't know…"

Quickly, the doctor examined Con.

Jessica burst into tears. "He was awake, I swear he was awake." She stared at Con's sleeping form. "Oh, my Lord, I hugged him. Did I make it worse?"

Dr. Wood smiled. "Probably not. The important thing is he woke up. What he needs now is sleep. And family when he wakes, so he stays anchored in the present." He gazed at John. "Just like we talked about."

John frowned at Jessica. "We were advised not to touch or hug him until we get Con's pain under control. Something to consider the next time he wakes up."

Jessica stared at him, horrified. The tears continued to flow. Oh, God, she had hurt Con.

Dr. Wood shot John a dirty look. "I'd say Jessica's reaction was perfectly normal. There was no way she could know what we'd talked about." He patted Jessica on the arm. "So, he spoke? Do you remember what he said?"

"Something like, *if this is heaven, I'm sticking around.* Then he groaned when I hugged him, so I stopped. He asked for water."

"And you think he knew who you were?"

Jessica shrugged. "He seemed to. I mean, he didn't appear confused when he opened his eyes." Jessica swiped at her eyes. "What happens now?"

"Now, we wait. Hopefully, each time he wakes, Connor will be a little more present. When he can stay awake for more than a few minutes, we can assess whether there's been any traumatic or brain damage." His eyes swept the family. "Until then, make sure he's never alone, and prepare to keep his brain stimulated. Music. Books on tape. Conversation. He needs to hear your voices. And remember, when people come back from a coma, even an induced one, there may be some sensory changes. For example, he may find certain smells irritating or complain his food tastes funny. Don't argue with him. Also, he may need to be reminded who you are, several times. Just roll with it. It may be temporary, but it could also be permanent."

Con sighed deeply. "My brothers always smell," he muttered, his voice still scratchy. His eyes remained closed, but he moved his head to the side. "Finn, Finn, the stinking nin." Con fell silent." Then he emitted a light snore.

Jessica giggled, then clapped a hand over her mouth. "I'm sorry. That was funny."

Moira smiled. "Don't you worry, my dear. When they were

little, Con used to call Finn a stinking ninny. Not very polite, but my boys seemed to delight in teasing each other." She gazed at the doctor. "So that's good, right? He remembers his brother."

Dr. Wood nodded. "Maybe. It could just be some sort of dream or a long-term memory. What he remembers in the short term will be more important." Wood shrugged. "He will probably have little outbursts like that until he's fully awake. Don't take them personally. He probably won't remember most of it. There is no way to predict where Connor has been in his mind or how it will affect him when he comes back.

"Be prepared for anything, and, as we discussed, let him talk. Without interruption. Don't push him to remember, don't interrogate him or correct him. Just let him recover in his own time." Dr. Wood fingered his stethoscope and wrinkled his nose. "And do not freak out if he doesn't recognize you. Be patient. This is more confusing to him than you."

Sadie put her hands on her hips and made a face. She pointed directly at Finn and sniffed. "It's not about you, it's about Con."

Jessica's mouth dropped open. What the heck was that about?

Finn held up his hands in protest. "Not sure why you're picking on me, but I understand."

Sadie crossed her arms and glared.

Con was confused.

He went toward the light, but when he got there, he didn't know the person waiting for him. He winced. She seemed to know him, since she called him by name. So why did he feel the immediate need to run? His brain was screaming at him to make tracks. So, he pretended to fall asleep.

Then he heard voices. Some he recognized, like the doctor

and his brothers. Others alarmed him. The females. They made him feel threatened, as if they meant him harm. He was afraid to stay awake. He needed to go back to where it was safe. The sponges. He needed the sponges. They made him feel claustrophobic, but they kept him safe. Oh God, where were the sponges?

Chapter Nine: Not Again!

Jessica turned awkwardly on the cot the hospital had provided. She had taken the late-night shift so Con's family could get some sleep.

Unfortunately, that was the shift that Con slept through. Moments of wakefulness mostly occurred during the day. Although Con seemed to know his family, Jessica still wasn't sure that he remembered her. That consumed her, though. "Have faith, right?" she mumbled as she turned to stare at the ceiling.

Con groaned, and she quickly went to him. They had been instructed not to speak first, because even though Con appeared to be awake, he might still be in a deep sleep. She gasped when he opened his eyes and stared directly at her.

"Jess? Right?" He sighed happily. "I wondered where you were. I was worried my family scared you away." His eyes closed, but then snapped open. "Or I made you up. But you're real and you're here."

Jessica smiled. She tried to hide her emotions. "I'm real. I encouraged your family to take the day shifts. They're who's most important."

"No," Con said loudly. He then grabbed her hand and spoke emphatically. "No. I want you." He grew agitated. "Don't let them keep you away from me." His body began to twitch and jerk. "No, no, no, no."

Jessica grabbed the call button and pressed it but got no response. She dropped Con's hand and rushed out into the hallway. "Help, someone, please."

A head popped up behind the nurse's station and an alarmed woman jumped up and ran toward her.

Jessica did not wait for her. She stared at Con's twitching body, feeling hopeless.

The nurse rushed in and ran to Con's bedside. Quickly, she lowered the safety gate and turned Con on his side, away from all the machines monitoring his condition. She gazed at Jessica. "I need you to keep all of those leads out of the way. My job is to prevent him from injuring himself."

Jessica nodded. She had heard about seizures, but she had never witnessed one. Gently, she gathered the cords and pulled them away from Con. Gradually, the tremors stopped and Con relaxed.

The nurse stroked his hand. "Connor? Can you hear me?"

Con opened one eye and stared at them. Then he moaned. "Head hurts." He shifted onto his back and closed his eye.

The nurse quickly checked the machines and muttered something to herself. She wearily shook her head. "I have to call the doctor. I'll be right back."

Jessica's eyes rounded. "What if…" Was this nurse really going to leave her alone?

"We're short-staffed tonight. Just keep watching him. I'll be right back, I promise." She scurried out of the room.

Con grabbed her hand. "Sorry. Scared you, huh?" He tried to laugh. "Me, too."

Jessica absently made the sign of the cross. "Sweet Lord, you scared the life out of me. It's bad enough you're in pain…"

The nurse rushed back in with a syringe. After she tapped it with a finger, she smiled at Con. "The doctor has ordered something for your headache. It will probably knock you out again. Dr. Wood will be here in the morning to check on you."

Jessica glared at the nurse. "But what about the seizure?"

"Not unusual in trauma cases. It could have been triggered

by a migraine or just prolonged pain. We will check him regularly for the next eight hours, but I've seen this before. Hopefully, this medication will ease the pain and silence the seizure reflex." She wiped Con's arm with antiseptic and stuck the needle in. He winced but said nothing. "This should quickly take effect. Just relax and sleep." She stepped back, watched him for a minute, then left the room.

Con focused on Jessica's face and again reached for Jessica's hand. "Before I pass out…" He paused and took a deep breath. "I want you to know how sorry I am about…" He huffed and breathed again. Then his eyes closed. He fell into a sound sleep.

Jessica waited until he snored softly, then gently released his hand. She returned to her cot and slept.

Whew. That was a close one.

That woman was there again. At least he knew her name. Jess. His mom and his brothers talked about her all the time. Like he and she had some sort of connection. How could he tell them he didn't remember her?

His mother was planning their wedding, that much was clear. And his brothers kept making jokes about *the old ball and chain*. Damn, they were making him uncomfortable.

Jess was a pretty woman. He liked her laugh. Obviously, she was devoted to him. She visited every day and talked about random things. Things he was hearing for the first time. Sometimes, she slept in the bed beside him. He'd awake and watch her sleeping. So peaceful. Like an angel.

Maybe that was what she was, because he really didn't remember her. All he knew was what others told him. Strange that he remembered everyone but Jess and her friend, Sadie, the girl with pink hair. That was why he couldn't wake up fully while she was around. He didn't want to admit he didn't remember her. How could he marry someone he didn't even know? That was baffling. Maybe he'd had feelings for her once, but he didn't anymore. He wanted to tell someone, but who? Would anyone really understand that a woman he viewed as a stranger was in his room, acting like she loved him? It was so freaky. Like that movie about the woman obsessed with a guy, so she boiled his rabbit. Thank God he didn't have any pets, at least not that he could remember. What person boiled pets anyway?

Often, Con just lay there. Pretending to be asleep. Listening to comments people made. He'd learned enough to fake it. And when he couldn't, he'd claim he had a headache, and they'd leave him alone.

But Jess, she was a problem. Sure, she was pretty hot. But she seemed kind of uptight. High-strung. Not his type at all. Whatever had he seen in her? Clearly, he would need to let her down gently, when the time was right.

Days swiftly turned into weeks. Con's recovery was slow, filled with positive steps and negative setbacks. The night shift yielded few conversations, since that was when Con slept. Jessica had no opportunity to exchange any more than a few words with him.

Sure, he smiled at her, and occasionally, she would feel his eyes scanning her body. But the words had been few, and it worried her. Jessica's shift consisted mostly of sleeping and sneaking snacks from the Nurse's Station. When the sun rose, she left the hospital and went back to her apartment to get ready for work. However, one thing was clear—something was not right with Con. He didn't remember her. She was sure of it. Not once had he mentioned their night together or what had happened since. Everyone else thought she was exaggerating, that she expected too much too soon. She had been advised to be patient. So she kept her mouth shut when Con seemed to have trouble recognizing her. How much longer would she have to wait?

"Jessica. Wake up, sweetie." Why did her mother always wake her on Saturday mornings?

Jessica huffed and sluggishly opened her eyes. "I'm coming, Mom." She groaned as she sat up. Slowly, her eyes focused and her mouth fell open. "Oh, Moira. Sorry, I must have really been out of it." She stared at Con's bed. It was empty. "Where's Con?" Panic consumed her. "Oh, no. Did he? Oh, my Lord, I fell asleep and he? This is all my fault."

Moira smiled. "No, no, no. Settle, dear. Con is getting an MRI, and when he returns, they will start removing some of his bandages. We'll finally get to see the damage done to that beautiful face."

"Oh." Jessica yawned. "I'm so sorry I fell asleep. I was just so tired." She yawned again.

"No worries. You both needed some sleep. I'm feeling grateful that Con slept the night without having another seizure." She hesitated. "It may be a while before we know the long-term effects of the beating. The doctor gave me a whole list, everything from personality changes to anxiety, sleep disorders, and so on. Apparently, those changes have no explanation, but the doctor ordered the MRI to see how Con is healing. They're still worried about brain damage because he isn't talking much and is always sleeping. We aren't seeing the happy Con we once knew. My son is now much more subdued."

Jessica made a face. "I'll admit, Con and I connected in the short time we knew each other, but I don't know him well enough to know what's normal and what's not. That seizure nearly scared the life out of me. But at least if it happens again, I'll know what to do."

"I imagine we will get a Bible full of instructions before we can take Con home."

"Have they said when that will be?"

Moira shook her head. "The doctor wants him in the hospital when he first talks to the police. So I imagine it won't be until Con is ready to be interviewed. So far, he hasn't said much about the attack or what happened after. I'm not sure he recalls it." She offered a slight chuckle. "He seems to know us, but I'm not really sure if he remembers everything about us. Sometimes, he just looks confused."

Jessica frowned. "I think he's been having strange dreams, too. He's been mumbling about sponges and angels and witches. Baffling things. I did some research on comas. Apparently, your reality can veer out of control. People you love become evil, normal situations lapse into horrendous tragedies. Everything seems exaggerated or contorted. Your mind is trying to deal with the lack of stimulation, and goes…well, apeshit." Jessica blushed.

Moira chuckled. "What a perfect way to describe this situation. Ape Shiite."

Jessica yawned. "If you don't mind, I'm going to nap until Con gets back. I need a few more hours before I head into the office."

"Oh, go right ahead, dear. I just might do the same."

Jessica was brought back to consciousness by Dr. Wood's angry voice.

"What the hell do you mean, he was taken for an MRI? I said I didn't want any tests until I examined him." He glared at a young nurse who looked like she was about to burst into tears.

"But you called and ordered an MRI. You said you wanted the results when you made rounds this morning."

"I don't do rounds, dammit. I'm not a hospitalist, I'm a neurologist. Someone other than his attending ordered that

MRI and I want to know who."

The nurse wrung her hands.

Moira pulled herself out of the armchair in which she had been napping and snapped, "Oh, stop carping at the poor girl." She sent the doctor a stink eye. "What are you belly-aching about, anyway?" She turned to Con's empty bed and frowned. She checked her watch and paled. "Has something happened to my son? He's been gone over three hours. Isn't that a little long for an MRI?"

Dr. Wood closed his eyes as if to calm himself. He sighed deeply and ran a hand through his hair. "This woman lost him."

Jessica sat up and stared at him. "What do you mean, she lost him?" She tried to combat the sick feeling invading her gut.

The nurse flushed, then turned toward the doctor. She straightened her spine and in a voice that dripped with anger, said, "I. Did. Not. Lose. Him. When the MRI tech didn't call me for a pickup, I went to the lab to check on Mr. O'Brien myself. He wasn't there. The tech said someone picked him up a while ago. I was about to call security when you started yelling at me for no damn reason."

Jessica shook her head. "Does this mean Con is missing? *Again?*" Dr. Wood nodded, and Jessica slapped her forehead. She muttered, "This isn't real. I'm dreaming. I've got to be dreaming." She lay back down and closed her eyes. "Go back to sleep. When you wake up, Con will be here. He'll remember you. Everything will be fine." Then she opened an eye and winced. Oh Lord, this *was* real. She sat back up and rubbed her eyes.

Dr. Wood ignored her. He scowled at the nurse. "Get security in here, *now*."

Moira chuffed. "Are you telling me you truly lost my son? You don't know where Con is? How is that possible? This is a hospital." It was clear Moira's fury was rising. "How the hell did you lose a man recovering from such serious injuries? It's not like he could walk away."

The intercom system crackled, and a voice said, "Attention, all staff, Code Green, Code Green. We are now in lockdown. Report per procedure."

A security guard appeared in the room. "I need a name, physical description, condition, any other identifying details regarding this patient."

The air in the room shifted. Jessica noted the panic in Moira's eyes, the concern in Dr. Wood's. *What the hell was going on?* Before she could respond, Dr. Wood began reciting the details.

"Patient, Connor Sean O'Brien, white male, fit, blue eyes, dark brown hair, a little over six feet tall, immobile. Tattoos on both shoulder and right arm, what they call *a sleeve*. Bandages on face and upper body. Splint on right arm, soft brace on left leg. Experienced heavy trauma to head and body as the result of an aggravated assault. Taken from his room three hours ago on orders from unnamed clinician. Taken from nuclear lab about an hour ago. Tech assumes pickup was by hospital employee."

The guard repeated the information into the communications device on his shoulder. "Houston and Lovell, begin search in Quadrant Nine. Meadows, run video starting approximately two hours ago at the Nuclear Lab. Let's see who removed the patient and where they took him. Landry, put the sheriff and chief of police on standby. Get moving, folks. Let's find our patient."

Confusion clouded Moira's face. "I don't understand. Surely, someone just mistook him for another patient and brought him back to the wrong room?"

The security guard gazed at her. "Unfortunately, ma'am, before a patient can be moved, hospital staff must scan their wristband and confirm their ID. There is little chance of a mistake, at least by hospital staff."

She tilted her head and studied the man, her eyes filled with questions. "You're saying he was taken intentionally? By non-hospital staff? For what purpose?"

The guard shrugged, spoke, then stopped. He gazed helplessly at Dr. Wood, who stared right back. Finally, he said, "Let's not jump the gun. We already have plenty to worry about. My staff will do their job, and I assure you, they will do everything they can to find him." He tapped his shoulder com twice, then moved toward the door. "Just sit tight. I'll report back on the hour."

Jessica went to Moira and hugged her. "Don't worry, they'll find him."

Moira's eyes rounded. "What that man wasn't saying was Con could have been taken for any reason. Witness tampering. Organ harvesting. Human trafficking, even illegal pharmaceutical human trials."

Jessica stared at her. "What? That's crazy."

Moira waved her off. "You don't read the New York newspapers, dear. There's all sorts of stuff going on in healthcare that no one wants to talk about. There are all kinds of evil people out there who do despicable things. Sometimes, they're desperate people. Who wouldn't think twice about stealing a patient out of a hospital." She reached into her purse and pulled out a rosary. "I never thought Con was the reason I'd wear out a rosary." She bowed her head and prayed.

Jessica stared at Dr. Wood. He appeared to be just as helpless.

True to his word, the security guard reported back on the hour.

After the first hour, the security staff confirmed Con had been removed from the MRI lab by two men who were not employees. At the time of the removal, the MRI tech was in his office, preparing the films for the doctor. He claimed to have seen nothing unusual about the men. After further questioning, he admitted he hadn't actually seen the men. They just called out that they were returning the patient to his room, and he didn't investigate further.

Using security cameras stationed at the exit doors, security tracked the men through multiple hallways and elevators. Finally, they wound up in the laundry room, where Con was dumped into a cart. From there, he was taken down several other hallways and to the loading dock, where a dark van awaited. Con was loaded onto a stretcher, quickly strapped down, and pushed into the back of the vehicle. The cart was left on the dock.

Dr. Wood was appalled at how roughly Con was treated. He was also angry at the failure of the hospital staff to notice a patient being wheeled through areas where patients were uncommon. "I can't believe not one person considered that strange and reported it."

Security's investigation yielded almost no helpful information. It was impossible to determine whether Con was the intended victim or whether he'd been snatched randomly. No one could verify why an MRI was ordered. In addition, there was no evidence that his wristband had been scanned at either location. "Why have security procedures when no one follows them?" Dr. Wood was livid. "This is a giant clusterfuck."

As the investigation continued, no one contacted the hospital. Neither the media nor the authorities claimed responsibility or reported anything unusual. Ultimately, the local police issued an alert for a vulnerable missing adult, including the description of the van and a partial license plate.

Con's family, as well as Jessica, a few police officers, and the hospital administrator were sent to a conference room, where they waited for news of Con.

Rodney Abbot, the hospital administrator, attempted to appease them. "I guess the good news is, the results of Mr. O'Brien's most recent MRI revealed some positive results. He is healing nicely, with no evidence of brain or irreversible organ damage. We believe his seizure was most likely triggered by one of his pain medications."

Moira growled at him. "The only thing I want to know is whether my son can survive being removed from the hospital. You had him hooked up to countless machines, especially life-sustaining ones. So I want the truth. Is my son's kidnapping going to be the death of him?"

Abbot shook his head. "I'm sorry. I can't tell you that. It may depend on your son's strength and his desire to live."

Jessica stared at him. What an idiot. She could not believe the man was attempting to cover his butt. She thought back to the last time she and Con spoke. Something was nagging at her. Something he had said? Or something she had seen. Her face screwed up in concentration. "Oh my God, what about the St. Christopher medal? Does anyone know if Con was wearing it?"

John frowned. "If he was, I imagine they would have removed it for the MRI."

"Except it was made of platinum, and that's considered MRI-compatible. It doesn't have to be removed. The magnet wouldn't mess with it."

Finn stood and gestured toward Jessica. "Let's check his room." He pointed at Abbot. "You get down to that MRI lab and do something useful. Look for the medal." He shook his head with a laugh. "I don't know how you're going to explain this to your board when you're sued for negligence, especially since the patient is a lawyer, as is his girlfriend."

Abbott paled but said nothing.

Jessica and Finn raced back to Con's room. They checked

the drawer in the nightstand, the closet that held other belongings, the bathroom, and in and around the bed. They found nothing.

Finn's phone beeped, and he checked it. "There's nothing in the MRI lab."

Jessica grinned. "So maybe we have some good news? If Con is still wearing that medal, perhaps we can track him."

Finn nodded. "Let's find out." He dialed what had become a familiar number. In a charming voice, he crooned, "Sheila, it's Finn O'Brien. Could you possibly run that locator chip for my brother again?" He paused. "Yeah, it's kind of urgent. My brother has gone missing again. However, this time, *we know* he was kidnapped." He harrumphed. "Yeah, when we find him, we should probably consider that, though he's not mobile on his own, so chaining him down might be overkill. For now, we need to know where he is."

Finn motioned to Jessica. "Write this down. Four three point zero zero zero, N, seven point, nine two one six w. Near Kosciuszko Park. Got it." He closed his phone. "What's Kozoosko Park?"

"It's on the south side of Milwaukee." Jessica frowned. "It's a really nice place. Kind of strange place to take a body."

"Or dump one. Come on, let's get moving."

Jessica whipped out her phone. "I'll alert Sadie and Syd. One of them is bound to be closer than us."

Chapter Ten: On the Road Again

"Ouch." Con winced as the vehicle in which he was riding went over a pothole.

He opened his eyes and swept his surroundings. Dammit, not again. Everything was fuzzy. He tried to focus. What drug had they given him this time? His head felt like he'd gorged on a case of beer. A cheap brand. And now he was back in an ambulance. Had he had another seizure?

The last thing he remembered was falling asleep in an MRI machine. Con forced himself to concentrate. Surely he was still alive. His body was riddled with pain, and he assumed pain was only for the living, not the dead. Instinctively, he closed his eyes again. *Keep your mouth shut until you understand the game.* He needed to get his bearings and figure out why he was in this…ambulance? Van? SUV? The vehicle hit something, and he squelched a laugh. Another pothole, yeah, he was definitely alive. There were no potholes in heaven. He was sure of that.

Con tried to tune into the driver. Was he with someone else or alone? He could hear someone talking, but he couldn't understand his words. He wanted to ask the guy to speak up. *Yeah, that would be a brilliant idea.* Slowly, his mind cleared, and he strained to hear.

"Time to stick the guy again. I don't want him waking up and giving us grief."

Another man snorted. "What's he going to do? Jump us? The guy can barely move. Someone beat the shit out of him. He must have really pissed off the Boss." He cackled.

"Besides, that's not our problem. Once the Boss takes delivery, I'm off to Cabo. Going to get me some tequila and Mexican pussy. Maybe go to one of those sex clubs. I hear things get pretty wild at those things. Lots of animal acts, if you know what I mean."

"Turk, that's disgusting. Stay out of those places. They see a drunk gringo with a fat wallet and anything might happen. You might be the one screwing an animal." The man's voice dripped with disdain. "I didn't know you were such a pervert."

Turk laughed. "Well, the Bosses' operation makes you think, doesn't it? Life is short. Then you die. You have no control over it. Figure I'm going to hell, anyway. Might as well enjoy the ride."

The driver groaned. "Well, sounds like all you're gonna do is shorten the ride." He sighed. "I'm getting out, Turk. That last job turned my stomach."

Turk pushed his seat back. "I dunno. The Boss said it couldn't look like a professional hit. It had to be messy, so the cops would think the guy had been knocked off by one of his homeless buddies. I wasn't expecting the guy to fight so hard. I figured we'd booze him up, he'd pass out, and we'd end him. I didn't think he'd fight back, and I definitely wasn't counting on his fingernails. Those things were so sharp, I was bleeding. I had to have my sister wipe me down with alcohol wipes. Told her I was attacked by a cat."

"Still don't know why the Boss went after a homeless dude. Far as I could see, the guy was just part of that gang that cleans people's car windows and then demands money. Not exactly a reason to off a guy."

"You know the Boss. He never tells us anything. Too low on the totem pole." Turk's voice moved closer. "How many needles should I stick him with?"

"One. Boss said he wanted to talk to him. We're not offing

this guy until then, as far as I know."

"That's because the guy is probably going to die, anyway. If you ask me, doping him up is stupid. Guy's on his last legs."

"Well, then don't. Not like the Boss will know."

Turk grunted. "Yeah, you're right." He moved away. "So, how you getting out?"

"Going to work for the Bosses' brother. I'm more a numbers guy."

"You're gonna be a bookie? Geez, you're gonna be so bored, you'll be begging me to take you down south."

"Naw, just trying to keep the wife happy. She thinks it'll be safer."

"Yeah, maybe."

A phone went off. Con heard Turk mutter, "It's the Boss."

"This is Turk, sir." He paused. "Yeah, picked him up about an hour ago. Been driving around like you said." There was silence, then Turk uttered, "Well, shit. How were we supposed to know that? He was the only guy down there." Turk ended the call and moved back toward Con.

Con kept his eyes closed as Turk tugged at his arm and looked his ID bracelet.

"Dammit, Harry. We snatched the wrong guy. Pull over, we gotta dump him."

"Are you shitting me? How is that even possible? We followed the Bosses' instructions to the letter."

"Except the guy's name was Arthur Von Bahm, not Connor O'Brien. We should have checked his wristband."

Harry was silent for a moment. "So, where do we dump him?"

"Boss didn't say. Look out the window, where we at?"

"Some park. Looks pretty empty. A few old guys wandering around, that's about it."

"Then pull over. We'll leave him on the curb. Someone is bound to find the poor sap." Turk patted Con's arm. "Sorry, man." He chuckled. "On the plus side, you get to live." The van screeched to a halt, and the gurney slammed against the back of the front seats.

Con wanted to scream out in pain but remained silent. A gush of fresh air hit him as the vehicle's back doors flew open. Suddenly, the memory of another vehicle hit him. Young boys bragging about their guns. Trash-talking about the owner of the convenience store. When he tried to intervene, the boys turned on him. Hit him. *Again, and again.* Left him for dead. Squeezer. Trying to help. Loading him into an ambulance...

Turk pulled Con roughly from the van. Although Con was strapped down, every movement inflicted more pain on his already abused limbs. He wanted to scream at Turk to be more careful, but he endured the pain with no comment. Finally, the stretcher stopped. Con was abandoned on the sidewalk. Turk and the van pulled away.

Con opened his eyes and sighed. The van was already halfway down the block. He was on his own. He had so many questions. What homeless guy was murdered? Who was Arthur Von whatever? He winced. Lord, his head hurt. Even trying to think was painful.

Con turned his head and surveyed the area. Okay, he knew this place. It was on his route. It was Kos...something Polish. Well, at least he knew it was a park. He winced again. Damn, his brain was working in slow motion. Like slogging through mud. Maybe he'd get lucky, and someone who knew him would find him. Con yawned. It was a nice day. The sun was warm on his face. Maybe he should just take a nap...

Con jerked awake. He heard footsteps. Was someone approaching?

"Hey, it's Saint. I heard he was missing."

Another man cackled. "Guess we found him."

"Ya think there's a reward?"

"Shut it, Lester. You're being greedy. That's how you wound up on the streets—by being greedy. If you hadn't gambled all your money away, you wouldn't be kissing a park bench at night." The man gently touched Con's arm. "Hey, Saint. Whatchya doing here?"

Con opened his eyes and groaned. He stared at the two disheveled men. "Lester, is it always about the money for you?" He took a deep breath, trying to fight the pain. "There may not be…an official reward, but if you call nine one one…I'll buy you free donuts…for a year."

Lester pulled on his unruly gray beard and snorted. "You already give me free donuts, Saint. Ya gotta up the ante." He waved his arms, his worn *Stones* shirt taut around his skinny body. "How the hell am I supposed to call nine one one? It's not like I have a phone."

Con shifted uncomfortably. "Can you loosen these straps, please? They're…killing me." He gazed at the other man. "Shifty, there's a church up the block. Run up there and…get a priest…or something?"

Shifty scratched his head and scowled. "Naw. That guy doesn't like street people. Caught some of them sleeping in his pews and chased them away in the freezing cold. Called them Milwaukee's shameful unwashed. Guess he doesn't know Jesus was homeless, too. He was one of the original street guys." Shifty rolled back on his heels and grinned.

Lester pulled on the stretcher's straps, which shifted Con's body.

Con bit his lip to prevent himself from screaming like a little girl. "Look, guys, unless you have recently…we need help." He tried to get comfortable again. "I'm a mess here. I need to get back to…back to…that place."

Lester peered at him and smirked. "Hey, Shifty. I think Saint's stoned. Listen to him slurring his words." He laughed. "Wish I had a phone to make a video."

Shifty shook his head. "None of that *what's good for the goose is good for the gander* shit, huh, Saint?" He huffed. "Don't be preaching to us about drinkin' when you're lying in the middle of a sidewalk stoned to the gills."

Con groaned. "Guys," he said more loudly. "Focus...find a phone and...call for help." In a frustrated voice, he said, "I need help."

Shifty shrugged. "Well, okay, Saint. No need to get pissed off. I'll find someone." He shuffled off, muttering, "There'd better be more than donuts coming, Saint.

Lester pulled hard at a strap. He almost tipped the stretcher. "Who the heck pulled these straps so tight?" He yanked hard again. "Maybe I should just cut the durn things." He searched through the dirty pants he was wearing. "Now, where did I put that?" He pulled out a pocketknife. "Here it is." He flicked it open and revealed a wicked-looking knife.

Con's eyes rounded. "Um, Lester. Be careful..." The last thing he needed was another cut on his body.

The air shifted behind them and Con felt another person approach. "Hold it right there, mister. You put your hands up and step away." Con turned his head and stared at a police officer, who had drawn a gun on Lester. Where had he come from?

Con blinked, trying to clear his vision. Yup. The policeman was real. "Officer, no need to overreact...I know this man..." Con gasped at the pain in his arms. "And he's trying to help me... Someone took me from the hospital and...and dumped me here." Con took a big gulp of air and coughed. "My name is Saint...uh..."

Lester glared at the police officer. "This here is Saint Con. The street lawyer? He's really hurt and needs help. You need to call for help. I would've, but I ain't got no phone." He held up his knife. "He wanted me to release those straps, but they're too tight, so I was gonna cut them." He narrowed his eyes. "Why would I hurt Saint? He's the only guy around here who tries to help us." He glared at the cop. "No one else does. You cops are always dragging us from our cribs, telling us to move on, like we actually have someplace to go."

The officer lowered his gun as another car pulled up. Sadie jumped out. At least it looked like her. Who else paraded around with pink hair?

"Dammit, Con. I rescued you once. I can't believe I have to do it again." She giggled. "By now, I've secured my place in heaven." She thrust her hands on her hips. "Besides, all of your shenanigans are killing Jess. You know, you can't just take a girl to the moon and leave her there. You suck at the follow-up."

Con tried to laugh, but it hurt too much. "Oh, stop. It hurts to..." He gazed at Sadie. "Hey, you got any bagels in your car?"

Sadie rolled her eyes. "Of course."

"Give some to Lester. He's the only one who has actually helped me today." He squelched another groan. "Damn...pain meds are wearing off..."

Sadie reached into her car and pulled out two bags. She handed one to Lester and the other to the police officer. She winked at the cop. "There's more where those came from. Look me up."

The red-faced cop gazed at her, then at Con and Lester. "Uh, thanks, I think." He hit the button on his shoulder com. "Dispatch, I need an ambulance at Kosciuszko Park, the Becher Street side. Somebody dumped a guy here, on a stretcher."

Sadie tapped him on the arm. "His name's Connor O'Brien. Saint Con. The guy who travels the city and provides legal assistance to the unhoused, the homeless."

The officer frowned. "The guy who was kidnapped and dumped in Burlington? How the heck did he wind up here?"

Con grimaced again as the pain in his head intensified. He was a lawyer? For the homeless? No, that was wrong. He was a priest. At least, he thought he was. "Wrong guy." He groaned as more pain struck his body. "Wanted Arthur…Von…Bahm. Kill him…And a homeless guy…Squeegee guy." Con struggled to keep his eyes open. *Do not pass out. Do not pass out.*

The sound of an approaching siren broke through the silence. Another squad car pulled up to the curb. This time, Con's family jumped out.

Fighting to remain conscious, Con blinked hard, then gazed at his parents and brothers.

Finn grinned at him. "I can hardly wait to hear how you explain this one. Mom's going to ground you forever."

Moira punched Finn in the stomach. "Stop behaving like you're ten." She ran to Con and tried to wrap her arms around him. "Jesus, Mary, and Joseph, my darling boy. Why does everyone want to hurt you? I'm not sure you're meant to be roaming out in the real world. Perhaps you should be confined to a seminary, after all." Methodically, she removed the straps around his arms. "There, at least now you don't look like an escapee from the loony bin. No son of mine will wear a straitjacket."

Con groaned loudly. "Thanks, Ma…straps…killing me." He closed his eyes for a moment, then opened them again. *Give me strength.* "As for the seminary…I thought I was…" He winced and shifted his body. "Wedding…supposed to be…a wedding?" He closed his eyes and groaned. "Stop…kidnapping me."

He opened his eyes, and his gaze moved to the police officer who had driven his family to the park. His voice was laced with pain. "Not the intended victim…this time…someone named Arthur…something…imagine they'll try…again."

Con paused and gritted his teeth. His head felt like it was

going to explode. "How…find…me?"

Finn grinned. "We used your St. Christopher medal, which I gifted you for your birthday eons ago, to find you. We tracked you here easily. Maybe you'd better keep it on you permanently, in case someone else tries to abduct you again." An EMT van pulled up to the curb. "As for the lovely Jess, she should be with those guys. You can talk to her about the wedding."

Jessica jumped out of the passenger side of the van. She stalked up to Con and glared at him. "I'm getting a complex. If you don't want to go out with me, just say so. All this cloak and dagger stuff is ridiculous." She exhaled. "I don't know how much more I can take."

"Jess…" Con groaned. "Can you please…" His eyes fluttered closed. His mind was drifting.

Jessica frowned at him. She moved to his stretcher. "What?"

Con reached for her hand. "Please…" He moaned, dramatically this time.

Jessica gazed at his family and cocked an eyebrow. "What?"

A female EMT stepped up to Con, gently brushed Jessica aside, and took his vitals. When she finished, she nodded at her partner. "He's good to go. Let's get him back to the hospital." She gazed at Con. "Do you want to go back to Burlington or someplace closer to home?"

"Saint…" Con named a hospital nearby. "Just want to…sleep." His eyes sought out Jessica's and he tried to smile. He wasn't even sure why he was smiling.

The police officer stepped forward. "I'm going to need a statement from you."

Moira harrumphed. "Get in line, mister. My son's not speaking to anyone until he receives medical treatment."

Con yawned. "What…ever."

Chapter Eleven: The Truth

Jessica stared at Con's sleeping form.

Since being rescued from the Milwaukee park, he seemed to sleep more, if that was possible. It was as if he was avoiding more than a basic conversation with anyone. And he was having nightmares. Violent, disturbing nightmares. He almost always woke up screaming. Con claimed to have no memory of the dreams, but Jessica was convinced they were about her and his family. Occasionally, he would call out names. Other times, he'd jolt awake and stare at them. Terrified.

When awake, his gaze was searching, as if he was trying to determine whether she was friend or foe. When he spoke to her, his words were clipped, his tone distrustful. The doctor advised the family to wait it out. Con's brain was trying to process both physical and mental trauma. According to the counselor the family brought in, he was having difficulty dealing with all of it. The cocky Con no longer existed.

His long-term memory seemed fine, but when Sadie's dad or Sydney brought up something that occurred in the recent past, something flickered in his eyes. She was sure it was doubt, as if he wasn't sure people were being truthful. And that meant it was possible there had been damage to his short-term memory.

His family didn't seem to notice. His conversations with them were normal, easy. He would chat with them for hours. With others, he was gracious and kind, but there was no real warmth behind his words. Any connection he had with others seemed to have evaporated into thin air. That was why Jessica was convinced he was pretending to remember. He was simply accepting what people told him. He remained silent about any doubts or questions.

That meant he really did not remember their one night together. The night she knew had rocked both their worlds and supposedly sealed their fate. The Con she knew then had been very vocal about his feelings. He had a plan for their future. He would take the steps necessary to get there. And he was not shy about public displays of affection. He had enjoyed touching her, kissing her, making suggestive comments. This Con allowed her to kiss him on the lips, but his response was tepid. He didn't flirt, and most concerning, he never once called her *doll*. While she liked the new Connor well enough, the spark between them had dissipated. This was not the man she had been falling in love with. No, this was not that man at all.

After two weeks of tending to Con, his parents reluctantly headed home. They were assured by hospital staff that their son was stable and well on his way to recovery. Although Moira objected, John insisted it was time for everyone to return to New York.

Con's release from the hospital was contingent on nighttime supervision. Jessica and Syd offered Con their third bedroom until the nightmares subsided, after he initially refused to have an aide in his home. Sadie wasn't happy about giving up the room she'd been promised, but quietly acquiesced when her father expressed his dismay at her selfishness.

Jessica and Syd were making a significant sacrifice by bringing Con into their home. However, Jessica was not sure she wanted to take responsibility for caring for him if he wasn't even aware of their former bond. In that case, he'd be living with at least one stranger, and that wasn't fair to anyone. There was no guarantee that their living situation wouldn't trigger more nightmares. More paranoia. The problem was, Jessica didn't know how to approach the subject. Everyone else thought Con living at her house was the perfect solution.

Sydney walked into the hospital room just as Con woke up. She smiled brightly and strolled to his bedside. As he sat up, Sydney enveloped him in a hug. "Hey, Roomie. It's going to be so much fun having you around. As long as you remember to put the toilet seat down, we'll be just fine."

Jessica smirked. "Did you buy those little foam fishies to make sure his aim is true? I don't want to clean up after him."

Con rolled his eyes. "Really? I'm not two. I can take care of myself." He grinned. "But I warn you, I'm a sleepwalker. My apologies in advance if I wind up in the wrong bed."

Sydney punched him in the arm. "Well, I sleep with a taser, and Jess has a baseball bat. If you wind up back in the hospital, that's all on you."

Suddenly, Con's face paled, and he was hyperventilating.

"Oh, crap." Jessica cupped Con's face in her hands. "Con, it's alright. You're safe. No one's going to hurt you. Now breath with me." She took a deep breath. "In and out. In an out." When he calmed down, Jessica glared at Syd. "Remember those triggers we talked about?"

Sydney's eyes grew wide, and she nodded. "Sorry, I was just making a joke. Con, believe me, neither of us would ever hurt you." She tugged on her long cornrows. "I'm getting your room in order. I went to your home and packed up some of your stuff. Your dad had someone wash down your food truck, and that's parked in your garage. When you need that, we can go over and pick it up."

Con gazed at her. "I have a food truck? What do I make? Tacos?" He frowned. "I don't remember knowing how to cook." He appeared confused, then tried to hide it. "No one mentioned a food truck."

Jessica stared at him. "Con, you were attacked in your food

truck. I thought you remembered that."

Con made a face. "I know I was attacked. Someone told me that. Until now, no one said anything about a food truck. I thought I was jumped on the street."

Jessica's mouth dropped open. No one had really talked to him about his mission as a street lawyer, either. He seemed to have recognized his clients in the park, so everyone assumed he remembered how he made their acquaintance. "Con, you know what you do for a living, right?"

"You just told me. I own a food truck."

Jessica inhaled a deep breath. She was right. He didn't remember. With growing uneasiness, she asked, "Con, who am I?"

Con made a face. "You're Jessica. I know that. From what everyone tells me, you're my girlfriend. The love of my life." He grimaced.

"From what everyone tells you? You don't actually remember?" Jessica studied Con. She hadn't been imagining it. He didn't remember. "How long have we been together?"

Con frowned. "Well, judging from all of those hot text messages we've exchanged, a while. When I got my new phone, I went back through all my texts. I gathered we were into sexting, and I can't imagine I'd do that with a stranger."

Jessica gazed at Sydney, dismayed. "And how did we get together?"

Con blushed. "Um," He shifted uncomfortably. "I'm embarrassed that I don't remember." He tried to smile. "Look, I may not remember how we met, but from what everyone tells me, it was love at first sight." He smiled. "Just because I don't remember every little detail doesn't mean I feel any less for you."

Jessica breathed slowly through her nose. This could not be happening. She persisted, "Con, how long have we been together?"

Con shrugged. "Does it matter? We're together now. Obviously, we're in love. Shouldn't that be enough?"

Jessica thought she was going to be ill. "Con, we met approximately four days before you were attacked."

He stared at her, stunned. "Then why the hell were we sexting? That's so not cool."

Sydney scowled at him and snapped, "Stop with the holier than thou bullshit, Con. You're not a priest anymore. You're not the morals police." She motioned between Con and Jessica. "You may not have been together long, but you were head over heels in love with Jess. You met her and you claimed her."

Con shook his head. "If we just met, why were you heading up the efforts to find me after I was kidnapped? Mom said you ran everything from your house. I thought you knew my parents. You got along so well together."

Jessica was on the verge of tears. He really didn't remember a thing. "We may have only known each other for days, but what we had was real. It was strong and passionate and overwhelming. As for why I allowed volunteers into my home for the search efforts—Sydney asked. And I agreed, because although I'd only known you for four days, we had one magical night. I wanted another." Jessica gazed at him. "Sure, it's not logical. But love doesn't have to be logical. All that matters is that two people meet, and their hearts, minds, and bodies connect. That is what love is." She studied Con. "But you don't remember that, do you? And you most certainly don't feel it." Jessica was devastated. She brushed at her wet cheeks and closed her eyes, trying to settle herself. Finally, she gazed at Sydney and said, "I'm sorry, I can't do this. You're going to have to find another place for him to stay."

Con tossed and turned in his own bed. In his own home.

He couldn't sleep. It had been five hard days since he was released from the hospital, and he still wasn't comfortable in his own bed. Something was missing. He just couldn't figure out what. It was as if he didn't belong here anymore.

Maybe his mother was right. It was time to go home. To New York. Back where his mother could arrange for care and he didn't have to deal with a nurse—a complete stranger—every time he had a raging nightmare. Nurse Emily was his mother's age and had a brisk air of efficiency about her. She came in at ten each evening, took his vitals, administered his medications, and literally put him to bed. Like a ten-year-old. If he got up during the night, she was there. If he had a nightmare, she was there.

Con didn't really know what she did while he slept. The house was always clean and the dishwasher empty. Otherwise, he assumed she napped, or read, or played on her phone. He didn't ask. By the time he awoke at eight in the morning, she was gone, the door locked behind her.

Two days a week, he went back to the hospital for physical and occupational therapy, then he visited his counselor. He sensed he was improving, both physically and mentally. Unfortunately, he could not even look at the food truck parked in his garage. Every time he saw it, he went into a meltdown. He started to sweat and fear consumed him. The air was sucked out of his lungs and he had to run. The nightmare of his beating and disappearance still plagued him. There had to be a better way to serve the homeless, maybe from a car or on his Harley. Or maybe he should just switch gears and go to work for a clinic or law firm.

He and the counselor had talked extensively about his options. She suggested taking on a partner to ease his transition back to working on the streets. The problem was, Con no longer felt safe. A partner would not change that. Strangers especially set off warning bells, whether he was at Mass, the grocery store, or the park. Crowds freaked him out, yet he couldn't stand being alone. For the first time in his life, he was considering purchasing a gun. The problem was, owning a gun terrified him more than facing one. Could he actually shoot someone?

At the rumble of the mail truck, Con went to his front door and waited for his mail delivery. Woody had been his mailman since Con originally moved into his Southside neighborhood. He was a friendly face in a sea of suspicious strangers.

Woody smiled at him and reached into his mail sack. "Got a package for you today, Saint." He made a face. "From some fancy jewelry store in New York. What's a matter? You couldn't just go to the mall like everyone else?"

Con frowned. "I don't remember ordering anything. Maybe it's from my mother or one of my brothers."

Woody shrugged. "Well, the package is insured. You must sign for it. So, it must be worth a pretty penny." He handed Con an electronic signature machine and a stylus. "Sign here." After Con did so, Woody handed him the small box and a few letters. "You have a good day now."

Con nodded. He studied the box. It was from Tiffany's. Occasionally he ordered gifts for his mother from there, but he couldn't remember any recent purchases. With a deep sigh, Con set the letter aside and walked stiffly to his kitchen to get a knife. He cut through the mailing tape, pulled out the packing, and found a small jewelry box. Curious, he flipped it open. Inside was an intricate silver locket shaped into a heart. It was inscribed, *You hold my heart.* Inside was a space for a photo.

Con's face screwed up in confusion. What the hell? It seemed like a strange gift for his mother. She didn't wear necklaces. After the removal of her thyroid, she hated the feel of anything around her neck, even a scarf. He would more likely buy her a pin or a totchke, like one of the angel figurines she favored.

A quick knock on the door brought Con back to his front door. He peeked out the side window. Syd. He opened the door. "Hey, I wasn't expecting you today."

Syd shrugged. "I was hoping Jess was going to change her mind, but she isn't budging. I brought back some of your stuff, in case you need it." She frowned. "Jess insists it hurts too much to have you around. I guess not remembering her and the night you shared is just too hard." She made a face. "I'm so sorry."

"I get it, I really do. From what she's told me, we had a magical night, and it doesn't help that I told everyone I know that I'd met the love of my life." He stroked his scruff-covered chin. "I wish I could remember. I've been trying to remember. The doc says it will come back when I stop trying." He shook his head. "I just hope I don't remember ten years from now, when it's too late."

Syd rolled her eyes. "Now that would really suck. I was so happy you guys were together. You fit, you know? I'd never seen Jess so hopeful." She sniffed. "She suspected you didn't remember. My question to you is why not just admit it? Why were you faking it?"

"People just assumed I remembered my life, so it was easier to go along. As I got better, I just started paying attention. Some things were new to me, others I finally remembered. But Jess, that's just a black hole, which has me questioning our whole relationship. Everyone says it was love at first sight, but that's baffling. I only knew her for four days. Sure, I like Jess. She's been great to me, especially considering the circumstances. But I don't feel like I know her. There's no sense we bonded, so we're friends, at least. There's no passion and at the risk of denying my manhood, no butterflies."

Syd stared at him. Her face screwed up in disbelief. "You don't remember the flowers? The late-night phone calls? The sexting? You told anyone who would listen that you'd met *the one.* Jess was the one who was skeptical. You were all in. You had no doubts. You were doing everything you could to convince her." She grinned. "From what she shared, some of your late-night calls were pretty hot. Made me glad I had the bedroom on the other side of the house. No way did I need to listen to that."

Con ran his hand through his thick hair. "Why can't I remember that? You'd think it would be imprinted on my brain." He sighed. "I'm not a player, I know that. Not like my brothers."

Syd shrugged. "Not a player, but charming as hell. And you thoroughly charmed Jess. You were her Prince Charming. In a few short days, she believed in love again." She pushed past him and dumped two duffel bags on the floor. "I don't know how you can get those memories back, Con. But I keep praying for a miracle. That girl deserves love. She deserves *you.*"

Slowly, Con panned the items he had set out on the coffee table as he FaceTimed his mother.

The first was the silver locket. Second was a gold claddagh ring with a large emerald heart and diamonds on the band. The third was a platinum bracelet with a Trinity knot. And the fourth was a key chain shaped into a *Serch Bytho*l, the symbol of eternal love. "I don't know, Mom. At first, I thought maybe I had bought these for you, which seemed a little weird, but I checked my credit card bill. They were all purchased after I met Jess, but before I was hurt. I don't remember buying any of them. Obviously, I went on some sort of spending spree. I wish I could remember why."

"Well, they're all symbols of love in some fashion. But not the same love you have for a mother. These are gifts signifying a commitment and true love. The emerald in the ring even matches Jess's eyes. It almost looks like an engagement ring. Obviously, you had strong feelings for her." Moira frowned. "Have you been in touch with her son?"

Con scratched his chin. "Nope, I burned that bridge. Once I admitted I didn't remember her, she was gone. Doesn't want to see me. Won't talk to me. I may not remember her, but I miss her."

Moira pursed her lips. "I have an idea, but I know how much you hate it when I butt in."

Con withheld a groan. Allowing his mother to interfere in his love life was troubling, but she usually had good advice for his brothers. He sighed deeply. "Let's hear it."

"When age chills the blood, when our pleasures are past. For years fleet away with the wings of the dove. The dearest remembrance will still be the last, our sweetest memorial, the first kiss of love." Moira offered a sweet smile. "The First Kiss of Love, by Lord Byron. Your father read the entire poem to me after our first kiss. Everything he says is true. You never forget the first kiss with the one you love. It plays over and over in your head. I remember it like it was yesterday. And I remember it every time your father makes me angry and suddenly, I'm not so angry anymore."

"Mom, I'm sure I wasn't Jess's first kiss."

"But was it the first kiss with someone she loved? I know it's so. Her friend, Sadie, told me all about your first kiss. She said Jess was overwhelmed, and I suspect you were, as well. That's why you pursued her."

"So, I'm supposed walk up to her, swing her body into a dip, and kiss her, like in the movies? Do you know this woman? She'd probably accuse me of sexual assault. Or kick me in the groin."

"Maybe. Maybe not. You won't know until you try."

"How am I supposed to try? Did you miss the memo? She wants nothing to do with me."

Moira huffed. She pointed at him imperiously. "You find her and kiss her, dammit. If you don't remember that first kiss, then move on. This cannot go on. It's time to shite or get off the pot, my dear!"

"Mom!" Con's face reddened. "I'm telling you, this is out of my control. There is nothing I can do to change it."

"That's where you're wrong, and you know it."

Con stared at her. Could it be that easy? He wanted his life back. Maybe if he could remember, he'd want Jess back. If all it took was a kiss, then dammit, he was going to try.

Chapter Twelve: The Kiss

The country-western bar was located off the freeway on a frontage road.

Sadie had promised Con that she and Syd would get Jess there. Apparently, Jess loved to line dance. It wasn't the best setting for romance, but it wasn't the worst, either. Con figured all he had to do was ask Jess to do the two-step and end the dance with a kiss. If he was lucky, he'd remember what had started their love affair and why those four days had mattered to the both of them. He knew this was his last chance to remember. He felt it in his gut.

For a while, Con stayed out of sight, sipping some local microbrew. He was watching the three women hoof it through The Hustle, the Electric Slide, and The Chicken Dance. Then the band shifted to Happy People by Little Big Horn and people coupled up for the Texas Two-Step. Con quickly deposited his bottle on the bar and moved toward Jess.

He doffed his black cowboy hat and bowed quickly. "May I have this dance, Miss?"

Jess stared at him. A second passed as she pursed her lips. Another second, and then a third.

Con wanted to beg, but he kept his mouth shut. Instead, he waited patiently.

Finally, Jess shrugged. "What the hell." She grabbed his hand and pulled him onto the dance floor. They stepped and turned, stepped and turned. They moved quickly, their arms instinctively winding through the positions.

Con winced as the pain in his head bloomed. The faster

they moved, the sharper the pain. Then something in his brain imploded. Con moaned loudly, wobbled, and slowly sank to his knees, holding onto his head. The couples dancing around them stopped and stared.

"Hey, man. You okay?"

"Con, what's wrong?" Jess kneeled down beside him and pulled him into her arms.

Con gazed at her. His eyes widened. Through the pain, memories of Jess came rushing back. Like a fast-moving video, it all came back. Meeting Jess. The first time they made love. Talking on the phone late into the night. The sexting. Accompanying the images in his mind were the feelings. The intense, overwhelming love he felt for this woman. Jess. His lovely Jess. He whispered, "Doll? What are you doing here?" He shuddered and his eyes rolled back into his head. Then he collapsed against her.

Jess held Con against her body and screamed. "Someone, please call an ambulance. We need help."

Syd appeared next to her and motioned at two men. "Help me get him into my car. There's a hospital a few minutes away. An ambulance will take too long."

She nodded at Sadie. "Call the hospital. The one on south Twenty-Seventh Street. Tell them we're on the way."

Sadie frowned. "Fine, but shouldn't he go back to…"

"Just do it." Syd glared at her, then paused as the two men awkwardly lifted Con's unconscious body and headed to the door. "Jess, come with me."

The two men helped Syd slide Con into the back seat. It wasn't easy. Con's body was dead weight. It had to be like lifting a large, heavy tree. She closed the door and jumped into the front seat.

Jess slowly lowered herself into the seat on the passenger side. "Syd, he called me *doll*. I think he's remembering." She choked back a sob. "I'm *sure* he remembered. Oh God, what if it was too much?" She brushed at her tears. "Dammit, it's my fault. I wanted this too much. I wanted him to remember. I prayed and prayed that he'd remember." She hiccupped. "But I didn't want him to die doing it."

"Did he have a headache? Did he complain about being in pain?"

"No, oh, I don't know. It happened so fast. He winced, then grabbed his head and fell to the floor."

"Dammit, that can't be good." Syd's tires squealed as she pulled out of the parking lot. "I'm taking the frontage road. That will take us right to the hospital. The freeway takes us too far east."

Jess nodded. "Yeah." She turned and gazed at Con. His face was ashen, his eyes closed, and his body so still. She bit down on her lip to stop crying. This was so unfair. Tonight, she finally felt hopeful again. When she'd spotted Con at the bar, she knew he was there for her. Whether or not he remembered, he'd come for her. She couldn't live with herself if this was how it ended. Jess reached back and grabbed one of Con's hands. "I love you, you know? When you couldn't remember me or what occurred between us, I didn't know what to do. How to move on.

"The first time you disappeared, I thought I had imagined everything. That maybe everything we had was one-sided. Then when we found you, I thought maybe God had brought you back to me because we belonged together. The second time you were taken, I thought my heart would break. How could God be so cruel? Especially to a man who has served him and done so much good? Then we found you so easily, I thought maybe God was protecting you.

"And when you finally admitted you didn't remember me, it hurt so badly I didn't think I would ever fall in love again. I felt so lost, so broken, so unloved by the God I had poured my heart out to. I begged. I pleaded. I negotiated and bargained.

The loss was so cruel. What kind of God punished people like that? What did I do to be punished like that?

"Now, this. I can't bear it. Your death or anything else is simply unacceptable." Her voice rose in anger. "Do you hear me, Con? Your death is unacceptable." She squeezed his hand. "If you're seeing that damn light, the one everyone claims to see when they're on the verge of death, you refuse to walk toward it. You stay here with me. You come back to me. I will not let you go."

Jess gasped when Con's eyes slowly opened. He tried to smile but grimaced instead. "Jess? I remember everything. From our first kiss. I'll *never* forget our first kiss." He frowned and tried to sit up. "My head hurts. It feels like it's going to blow apart. What happened?" He winced as his eyes closed and he fell silent.

The car lurched to a stop. Jessica replied softly, "We don't know, but we're going to find out."

Syd jumped out of the car and began yelling for help.

A woman dressed in scrubs rushed out of the emergency entrance, hauling a gurney behind her. Two men, also dressed in scrubs, were with her. Quickly, the woman yelled out instructions and helped the men place Con on the gurney.

Jessica gazed at her, surprised. "Mrs. English?"

The woman was startled, her gaze fierce. "Jess, do you know this guy? What happened?"

"This is Connor O'Brien. The street lawyer? The guy that was beaten up, then disappeared. The one Sadie found?"

"Oh, that's why Sadie called me directly. She told me someone was headed this way, but then she started babbling about you and your true love. I finally had to hang up on her." She shook her head. "Her mother is an emergency room nurse, and that girl loses her marbles when there's an emergency. It's a good thing she works in bagels." Mrs. English nodded at the hospital staff. "Let's get Mr. O'Brien inside.

Jess, you stay with him. Syd, you come with me."

Con smiled at Jessica.

She was curled up in a chair bed, sound asleep. "Jess? You awake?"

Jessica started. "What?" She scrubbed her face with her hands. "Oh, Con. You're up." She shifted on the bed. "What time is it?" She gazed at him. "How's your head?"

Con shrugged. "Well, the headache's gone."

Jessica nodded. "Good. The doctor called it an acute migraine. He said it's not uncommon for people who've had memory issues due to head trauma." She yawned. "Not sure what they gave you, but it knocked you out. They said they'll prescribe something in case it happens again." She studied him. "How's the memory?" Carefully, she added, "Do you still remember me?"

Con shot her a leering grin. "Yup, Doll. I remember everything, from the moment you bumped into me with your lip gloss to the way you seduced me into your bed and those cute little noises you make when you come. I mean, who giggles through an orgasm?"

Jessica blushed. "Me, apparently." She stretched and yawned. "What I remember is how aggressive you were when we met. You were not about to take no for an answer. You were not to be denied."

"Huh. I thought I was irresistible. I think you said that when we were sexting."

Jessica giggled.

Con arched his eyebrows. "Giggles, already? Damn, I'm good. I haven't even touched you yet." He crooked a finger. "Come here, doll." He pointed to his lips. "These need some attention, and I'm kind of held captive by the IV."

Jessica peeled herself from the sleep chair and moved to the hospital bed. Con raised his blanket and waved her under it.

When she slid in next to him, he rolled on top of her and kissed her deeply. Yes! It was there. The sparks, the flames, even the damn butterflies. Everything he remembered. How could he have forgotten this? Con's tongue slipped into Jess's mouth while he palmed her breast. Oh God, it felt so good. He couldn't even be embarrassed because he was humping Jess like a teenager.

"What the hell? Don't you two know better than to have sex in a hospital bed?" Mrs. English shouted, shaking her head in disgust. "You set off the IV alarm. Did you think all that beeping was your heart?" She pointed at Con. "I'm pretty sure those meds do nothing for the libido, so don't even try to blame that. Now cover yourself up. I'm too old to get excited by your naked but well-toned butt." She turned to Jess. "Get dressed. I'm waiting for the doctor to give me your release papers." As Mrs. English left the room, she slammed the door closed.

Jessica laughed. "Now you know where Sadie gets it from."

"At least she has good taste. She said my butt was *well-toned.*" When Jessica tried to sit up, he pulled her back down on the bed. "Get back here, woman. I'm not done tasting you."

Jessica shook her head. "Nothing worse than a horny Saint."

"I told you, doll, even saints have sex."

Jessica smirked. "I know."

Con shot Jessica a wicked smile.

"It's time for some afternoon delight." He pulled her closer. "As I remember, it all began on this very couch." He shifted so he was lying on top of Jessica.

Jessica snorted. "You are avoiding a much-needed

conversation."

Con planted kisses across her neck to her mouth. "We're talking."

Jessica attempted to pull away from him. When he wouldn't unhand her, she squawked like a chicken. "Someone is too chicken to have an adult conversation."

Con glared at her. "Woman, I'm trying to seduce you. That's as adult as it gets."

Jessica clucked again and pushed at his chest. "Do I look stupid? You may be all hot and sexy, but don't you dare use that to avoid the conversation we need to have."

"Yes, I'll marry you. You're wearing my Claddagh ring. Surely you know what that means." He lifted her hand and kissed her ring finger. "And it's pointed in the right direction, so I know you haven't changed your mind about me."

Jessica's tone was stern. "Con, stop it."

"What? Is this about children, then?" Con chuckled. "I told you I will give you all the *bairn* you'll be wanting."

Jessica pushed him away and sat up. "First, you won't be giving me anything unless I agree to it." She arched an eyebrow. "My body is a temple, and while you may have permission to worship it, what I do with it is solely my decision. You need to remember that." Her eyes narrowed. "Now cut the crap, Con. We sold the food truck and bought a very nice van to replace it. Why is it still sitting in your driveway? Why haven't you used it to continue your law practice?"

Con mumbled.

"Excuse me?"

Con sighed deeply. What was he supposed to say? He knew everyone expected him to go back to being a street lawyer, but they didn't know about the nightmares or the constant triggers out there. When he and Jessica went to Brady Street for pizza, they'd passed the site of his beating, and he had a meltdown. At the beach, a group of rowdy dark-skinned teens walking in his direction freaked him out.

He was a bundle of nerves, and he just knew getting back on the streets would be a disaster. "Jess, I don't know what to do. I'm ashamed to admit that I'm terrified to go back to the streets." He shook his head. "My head is still a mess. My therapist says I have to work through my fears, but I'm afraid to do that. What if I can't do that?"

Jessica took his hand. "Let's look at the options. You could find a partner—another lawyer or paralegal who will work with you on the streets. You could find a storefront somewhere and use the van to bring clients to you. Or you could visit homeless shelters and soup kitchens rather than setting up in more public settings. Maybe you could even join a free legal clinic with the understanding you only serve the homeless." She pushed a lock of hair out of her eyes. "Or you totally shift gears and do something else."

"Like what?"

"Teach. Run for office. Start a youth program. Or a build a youth center." She smiled at Con. "I believe in you, Con. I believe you will continue to make a difference, no matter what you choose to do. You have been on an amazing journey so far. It's time for the next step."

Con frowned. "Doll, who am I if I'm not a street lawyer? If I don't help the homeless, who will?"

"For once, be selfish. What will make you happy? And even more important, what will make you feel safe?"

Con remained silent. His trust fund allowed him to do whatever he wanted. He didn't need to work. Clearly, his entire life was at a crossroads. The pending changes would be affected by whatever path he chose. Marriage, fatherhood, a need to serve. He wasn't an office guy. He knew that. What could he do that would feed his soul, but support major life changes like marriage and children?

Then it hit him. He gazed at Jessica and smiled. "I want to

share my story and the stories of those who fell between the cracks. I want to write and speak, maybe teach, about social justice. Why it's so important. Why we bear a responsibility to aid those in need. Provide a blueprint for others who want to heed the call. And I could use part of my trust fund to offer grants to organizations that benefit the unhoused, the hungry, people who fall between the cracks. Maybe even train and support some lawyers to work the streets. Share what I've learned. That's got to be worth something."

Jessica chuckled. "Wow, I was not expecting that. But you have the contacts and support to do all of that." She grinned. "Maybe we should sell the van."

"Oh, hell no. We're going to need that for all our babies."

Jessica snorted. "Okay, Mr. Sperm Donor. That van seats ten. You'd better hope men can get pregnant, because there is no way I'm popping out eight children."

Con grinned. "Well, maybe Finn and Danny will finally settle down and contribute some cousins."

EPILOGUE: TWO YEARS LATER

Con smiled at the crowd that filled the auditorium. Behind him, the stage was filled with graphics related to his first book, "Saint Con: The Journey Begins."

He had been surprised when asked to make the TED Talk. His book had sold moderately well, but the biggest payoff had been the opportunities to share his ideas. Articles. Interviews. Podcasts. Talk shows. Speaking engagements. People were listening, and that satisfied his soul.

Jessica, Syd, and Sadie, along with a marketing expert, started a foundation to support social justice education for the hungry and unhoused. When not writing, he served as a guest lecturer at local universities and law schools. Despite the occasional nightmare, he learned to better manage his PTSD with marriage, an impending family member, and a busy foundation. Hopefully, soon the only thing waking him at night would be his first child.

His eyes found Jessica, heavy with child, sitting in the audience. She gazed at him with pride and flashed a thumbs up. To observers, it was a sign of encouragement. To him, it was an assurance that their son was not planning to make an early appearance.

A member of the technology staff signaled it was time to begin. He nodded and placed the wireless mic behind his ear. With a big smile, he strolled to the center of the stage.

"Good evening, everyone. My name is Connor O'Brien, and I am pleased to be here to share my story.

"I emphasize the words *be here* because two years ago, my

survival was in doubt. I was working as a street lawyer then. On the day of my first date with my now wife, I was attacked at my mobile office and left in a cornfield.

"Once my friends and family learned I was missing, they began searching for me. Days after the attack, they finally found me in a hospital in Burlington, WI. In a coma. When I awoke, I not only suffered from partial amnesia, but also PTSD. Two things of note. The partial amnesia mostly concerned my now wife, Jessica. Although I knew when we met we would marry, after the attack, I didn't remember her. *At all.*" He shook his head. "That wasn't pretty."

"And second, when I was finally on the mend, I was kidnapped again." He smiled slyly. "I guess God didn't think I had suffered enough." The audience laughed.

"It turns out the two thugs who took me grabbed the wrong guy." Con grinned and peered upward. "Seriously, was no one in heaven paying attention?" Again, the audience laughed.

"Anyway, when it was discovered that I was the wrong man, I was dumped in a Milwaukee park. Two of the homeless citizens I served found me." Con smirked. "Neither of those guys had a phone. They couldn't call nine-one-one." He held out his arms and shrugged. "If you're looking for a good luck charm, I'm not it.

"The physical and emotional trauma inflicted by these events rendered me unable to return to my career as a street lawyer. I was just too afraid. Of being alone. Of dealing with strangers. Of anyone who resembled my attackers. Of any locations associated with the attack." He paused. "What do you do when you're so traumatized that your former life makes no sense?" He pointed at the large screen bearing a photo of his book. "You write." The audience applauded, and he bowed. "Thank you."

"While my dedication to social justice did not change, my

approach did. Since I no longer felt safe on the streets, I had to find another way to promote the cause. It occurred to me that although many people knew what *homeless* or *unsheltered* meant, they didn't really understand it. We've all seen the homeless begging for cash on street corners or sleeping in a park or camping under a freeway. But did you ever wonder how they got there? Why they were forced to live that way?"

Con cocked an eyebrow. "If you thought it was voluntary, you'd be wrong." A few people chuckled. Con shot the audience a stern look. "Your misconceptions about the unhoused do more harm than good."

A chart appeared on the screen behind him. "For example, did you know that one-third of the homeless are children? Individuals under the age of eighteen?

"That on any night in America, a significant number of the homeless are veterans, people who served in our military? Men and women who returned from war unable to readjust to civilian life?

"That only a third of America's homeless suffer from some form of mental illness?"

"We have permitted homelessness to persist because we excused it with myths of our own making." A photo of people of all genders, races and ages appeared behind him. Con scowled. "It's time to face facts, folks. A significant number of the people in our country are one paycheck away from homelessness. They and their families could be cast out into the street through no fault of their own.

"This is America. How can that be?"

A photo of Squeezer appeared on the screen. "Meet Squeezer, formerly known as Professor William A. Templeton. Ten years ago, he taught British Literature at a local university. Then his life imploded. His wife and daughter were killed by a drunk driver. Then he discovered that his mother had cancer. And to add insult to injury, the number of classes he was assigned to teach were reduced by half due to lack of student enrollment. The depression that followed was crippling. Squeezer lost his home. Then his car, which had become his new home. He sought assistance for his mental health, for food and shelter, but the system failed him. He fell through the cracks. He was denied benefits because he didn't have a permanent address." Con smiled. "After receiving treatment for his depression, Squeezer found work and was rehoused.

"Now he works for me."

A photo of a middle-aged woman with blue hair and dark skin popped up on the screen. "Meet Millie. Her formal name is Alicia Mildred Swenson. I found Millie sleeping on a park bench in New York City. Her story begins with the pandemic. When the restaurant where she worked as a line cook closed, Millie couldn't pay her rent. She and her disabled husband were evicted from their tiny one-bedroom apartment. Without enough money for rent and security deposits, she and her family resorted to sleeping outside.

A photo of a sweet teenager with long blonde hair and big blue eyes popped up. "Meet sixteen-year-old Caitlin. Caitlin went into the foster care system when she was ten years old." A rueful smile crossed his face. "She was adopted by a childless couple. For a while, she was safe and happy. Then she was molested by a neighbor, her new parents' preacher. Her parents refused to believe her story, so she ran away. She wound up on the streets of Houston, Texas. When I met Caitlin, she was living with several other teens in an abandoned building. She told me they had banded together to protect one another, and they moved almost weekly to escape the attention of pimps and drug dealers. Can you imagine having to live like that at sixteen?"

More photos popped up on the screen as Con reviewed the histories of seven other homeless people. When he reached the last, he said, "People aren't born homeless. They don't actively choose to be homeless. They don't deserve to be homeless. They aren't all drunks or addicts. Or criminals. Or mentally ill. Again, that's what we tell ourselves to avoid our obligation to our fellow man. It makes us feel better to judge the homeless unfairly."

He pointed at the audience. "I spent several years on the streets with the homeless and I can tell you they want what most people want. A roof over their heads. Regular meals. Safety. Opportunity. What's amazing to me is other countries—such as Finland, Iceland, and Japan—have found their own successful solutions to homelessness. In America, though, arguably one of the most compassionate and wealthiest countries in the world, we barely address it. That's disgraceful and what's worse, it's intentional.

"I don't care what religion you observe, or even if you don't. At the very foundation of humanity is our need to love and care for each other. To extend a helping hand when it's needed. Every one of us has the capacity and the ability to transform a life in a meaningful way. And every single American deserves the opportunity for that transformation.

"By now, I'm sure many of you are asking, what can I do? I'm only one person."

Con grinned. "I hope you don't think I'm going to let you get away with that." He pointed at the audience. "That's a cop-out. You and me, we're going to find a way to make a difference in the lives of the homeless.

"Here's my plan..."

About the Author

Award-winning author Seelie Kay writes about lawyers in love.

Writing under a nom de plume, the former lawyer and journalist draws her stories from more than 30 years in the legal world. Seelie's creative pen has resulted in more than twenty tales of contemporary and paranormal romance, and romantic suspense.

Seelie resides in a bucolic exurb outside Milwaukee, WI, where she enjoys opera, the Green Bay Packers, gourmet cooking, organic gardening, and an occasional bottle of red wine.

She is also an MS warrior and ruthlessly battles the disease on a daily basis.

Seelie can be found on most social media, including Twitter, Facebook, Instagram, and TikTok. To subscribe to her newsletter, please visit https://rb.gy/w69pim.

www.ingramcontent.com/pod-product-compliance
Lightning Source LLC
LaVergne TN
LVHW010108170826
845678LV00012B/2303